D1302247

. . . a hallucinatory love story that takes place in a twilight world of memories, where an "attempt to peel off the scab merely reopened the wound," continuing the author's work in the hallucinatory and elegiac—and always lyrical—vein of his earlier books. In this novel, which puts one in mind of James Joyce's *Ulysses* as much as William Burroughs' *Naked Lunch,* emotional contours are captured in prose that moves and glints like mercury, "lunatic and afraid of nothing."   —ERNEST HILBERT

The manuscript cover of Bernard's relatively short novel *Meditations on Love and Catastrophe at The Liars' Cafe* says it took almost five years to write, and any reader can understand why: its intellectual reach, the lapidary nature of its images and observations, the density of the writing are phenomenal. And yet such are Bernard's skills and literary exuberance that I was carried along on this avalanche, this onrush of ideas and images, and induced to read at a speed almost too fast to savor them. . . . I'm a fan of Bernard and have liked everything of his I've read, but I wasn't prepared for this. It's as though Bernard the intellect, Bernard the novelist and Bernard the poet had joined forces to produce one all-in-one, explosive synthesis. I kept wanting to underline favorite phrases and images, all the while wondering whether he could sustain this density, this inspired panoply of images. Indeed he could. His novel *A Spy in the Ruins* may one day earn the wider readership it deserves, but this book may accomplish that end first. It's probably considered "difficult" on the literary scale, but so is most of Nabokov, Shakespeare, or for that matter, *Moby-Dick.*   —CURT BARNES

OTHER BOOKS BY THE AUTHOR

NOVELS
A Spy in the Ruins
Voyage to a Phantom City

SHORT STORIES
In the American Night and Other Stories
Dangerous Stories for Boys

PLAY
The Beast and Mr. James

POETRY
The Rose Shipwreck:
Poems and Photographs
Chien Lunatique

Meditations on

Love & Catastrophe

at

The Liars' Cafe

A Novel

Christopher Bernard

A *Caveat Lector* Book

REGENT PRESS
Berkeley, California

Paperback
ISBN 13: 978-1-58790-514-8
ISBN 10: 1-58790-514-0

E-book
ISBN 13: 978-1-58790-515-5
ISBN 10: 1-58790-515-9

Library of Congress Control Number: 2019942455

An earlier version of this novel, titled "*AMOR i KAOS*," was serialized in the web-based monthly magazine *Synchronized Chaos*.

Source of images: PxHere (stock).

This novel is dedicated to the memory of the Spanish novelist Juan Goytisolo (1931–2017), whose example has given many the courage to follow the drive of imagination and desire wherever it leads, in fear and fascination and wonder.

> The Blind Rider,
> Count Julian in his pocket,
> Juan sin tierra on his eyebrow,
> Makbara at one ear,
> the Solitary Bird at the other,
> rides his blind horse over the blind country:
> a walk, at first slow,
> then a trot, faster,
> then a canter, faster,
> then a gallop, faster,
> faster, yet faster,
> till the blind horse
> opens his blind wings
> and lifts him
> on the stones of the wind
> into a blind
> sky.

. . . yearning brings forth its spectres.

— EGON SCHIELE

The wind rattling the kitchen window is suddenly clear as the shaking of a cage.

So you are not in love with me anymore.

Did he say those words or only think them?

Yet there is satisfaction, of a kind, in using his own hand to twist the blade.

She watches him, with a chilly pity.

—It's time . . . I lived past you . . .

The shaking seems to increase, though that may be only a result of shock.

But he shouldn't be surprised.

—Unfortunately for me, I am still in love with you.

His mouth is dry. His voice has the haughty intonation it takes whenever he is on the defensive. He barely controls the clot of rage closing his throat.

But, now that she is racing away from him toward where he can never reach her, has she ever looked more beautiful?

He feels an inane smile on his face and becomes intensely aware of how perfectly Sasha's eyebrows nearly meet above her small, childlike nose, her pale cheeks, the stung lips, as she looks gravely at him, and his coffee mug, suspended in midair, sinks down to the table with an almost noiseless sound, like the single tick of a clock. And, as it's said to happen when a person is drowning, his entire life—in this case, all the time he and Sasha have known each other—seems to flash, in random pieces divided by bitter dreams, before his eyes.

As he walked out of the snowy landscape into the bar, little more than a cube of shadows, called The Liars' Cafe (built after the demolition of The Philosophers' Club, where a hole had lain in the ground for many years before a local declared that a bar might burn, but it never went broke, and decided, optimistically, to rebuild), the sun stepped from the clouds, waved his hat, and withdrew. A crowd of eyes—almost exactly the same as those populating the vanished darkness of "Le Cloob," as it had been called by the regulars; now more haggard, more empty, more wistful—turned toward him from the battered counter like a host of flies, not unsympathetic but curious.

Grumbling, sighing, a dry laugh.

—Pascal, my boy (the portly man said, with a kind look), tell me it isn't so.

He had seen it in her face for weeks: defiant, sullen, distant, like coins falling down a well. The austere contempt around the mouth. At least she had dropped the vicious silences, heavy as attacks; it had seemed a consolation.

Someone else was nearby: a short, bald guy with spider glasses, a bully-type, behind the room divider.

The frost had come early; he'd walked across a mile of it to get here. The sun had been hiding behind a mask of gray wool flecked with crystals of ice sweat.

What he needed now was these random human sounds, grunts of noncommital sympathy, like the open strings of a guitar.

The buzzing immediately became softer, less itchy as it hummed. Like warm animals in a barn in the country where he grew up. Or damaged buses in a depot waiting for the mechanic's whistle.

Perhaps if he had been crueller, kinder, more needy, more independent, paid more attention, humiliated her, played the cat and forced her to wonder doesn't he love me anymore? there's nothing like doubt to make . . .

—Hey Manny! Look outside!

He couldn't have been there that long. But all of them could see the winter beginning once again to cover the world with its impure whiteness. Like an enormous bleached sheet falling in great blowing swirls from the gray, locked clouds.

—And there's nothing beyond but pitch black, he had told her once. She'd been right here, not two feet away, looking at him with her usual testing, exploratory expression.

—You wouldn't want me to go there, would you? Together? she said. Us?

Perhaps that was the moment it started to unravel: the question he failed to answer. Go to nothingness together, and settle there, as in a bee-loud glade, as in the poem.

He looked back across the whiteness.

Later, he'd gone on, in his usual thoughtless way:

—Because here, now, everyone can be seen, at all times, in all places. Naked, in theory, forever. So never despair. We're at least being paid attention to. Which is what everyone seems to want these days. Shame is no longer shame when shared with everyone.

She had been troubled by that, her privacy being her most prized possession. And then there was the colossal weight of a civilization moving, in a glassy delirium, as calm as a sleepwalker toward shipwreck. Though they both knew, about the future, uncertainty was the only security. Even if it was logically sure, by fiat or the rules of Fergus and the brazen cars, or all the signs rushing toward them like a herd of terrified horses.

That had been even longer ago.

—So, little wonder you were freaking out, my boy. To be detached is to be radically divine: beyond me, at any rate. It was the portly man again. What was he drinking?

17

The trail of tears some called it, and they knew of what they spoke. The barred lines, red, white, and black, painted across their cheeks, the lonely, angry eyes. The astonishing loss of their power.

Perhaps later he'll learn exactly what the doctrine they lived by was, but for the time being he had to resign himself to the memory of the horses in furious advance.

Lines of sailboats leaned into the wind, tacking toward some unknown reef snuffling in the surf in the northern inlet beyond the jetty.

—Point: The elegiac tablets in the archaeological exhibit excavated in Helmand after we Americans left. They gave away two millennia hidden between the lines of distressed text: exact accounts, awkward poems. Erased by a thoroughly scientific restoration.

—They were meant for a science gone crazy with success.

—You've got that right, Sasha had said with a triumphant smile. "Crazy" is the least of it.

—Then jihadists blew up the ancient cities, the ruins of our memories . . .

Clouds run over the horizon like the head of his beer, a blue, embossed cap taking over the sky, Merriweather's supreme promotion into the higher valleys. Cancelled tickets, overdrawn accounts, the banks running like fever blisters into fraudulent reconcilements.

Unearthed webs, slick and sticky with suffocated flies.

—Who is the master spider of the world wide web?

—We can't allow this. They can't allow it. You can't allow it. But you can't escape it.

They swindled the arcane agents, sanctimonious as CIA torturers. Something about it that . . . no (she said), don't say it.

—An inhuman low. No: a very human low.

—Eggshell. Minnow, Sasha murmured. Dryad. Blossom. Lucifer. Christopher!

—There are more where you came from, babe.

—Just a few seconds to flower. These berries are soft to the tongue and of just the right sweetness, she said, with a light drawl. Q. It's so lovely I am allowed to eat food. Breathe air. Feel the sun on my skin.

—A factory of genomes in the turf wars over the long sabbatical.

—Luckily (the portly man, piping up again, said), they didn't really matter.

—Who's they?

—Just they. Them.

Pascal sighed over his drink at the tavern window, overlooking, on this side (yes, it must have been yesterday, or the year before? last week?), the shabby avenue.

—I adored you. Really. Truly madly deeply, like in the old movie about the lover who comes back

19

from the dead. But God knows you made me pay for the privilege.

—Never, she whispered.

—Of course I couldn't escape, what was I thinking?

—Maybe it began in babyhood …

— … the obvious jeers, the templated, crafty betrayals discovered long after it was useless to take revenge. Perilous as window washing at the Windows on the World. So many guilelessly happy years ago. What is still amazing to me is that he walked so brazenly across that wire between the invisible towers. The ones piled up in the dim, candle-lit attic.

—A stroke, a shock, an ache. The stillness of the angels and the clatter of the spoons against the bars. Fading, windswept palms.

—Presumptuous tears.

—Then the industrialists were all over us. Though it wasn't just anybody, of course.

—Blame James Watt and his pernicious steam engine!

—De Jouffroy and his palmy Palmipède. Fitch and his pernicious Perseverance. Fulton's Folly. Edison. Ford. Hooligans. Confetti. Patricide, matricide, take your pick. The yellow wax buildup on the floor of a hopeless advantage. Rising into the space between the cocktail cabinet and the spring that never came.

—You understand my meaning?

—Maybe, but I don't want to play that hand yet.

—Another stroke and shock and ache.

He turned from the sheets rumpled on the floor.

Suddenly there seemed to be nothing behind Sasha's eyes.

—I'm the first to admit I do not have a clue.

Shelters at the bottom of the garden. A pool for ducks and geese. A shed. A hammer. A chalice. The chinks in the roof between the dirt floor and the sun. Empathy was held in common in that place.

—Act as though it were a living thing that needed you as much as you needed it. That doesn't sound too bad, do you think? Be nice to them and maybe they'll be nice to you. There are bloody exceptions. Who ever said love didn't require a certain detachment regarding your own precious skin?

—I won't live forever, he said, with a skinny laugh, so don't even think about it.

—Love is one of the luxuries. Live large and go when you must. Don't fool yourself into thinking you're going to survive. That's guaranteed to make you behave very badly. I've always found it comforting to know there are always more where I came from.

— I was referring to the cow. The one in the field. That is there now. Whether I think about it or not. What did you think I meant?

—He gets so preachy at times, but the goddam

bastard is sometimes right. Anyway, his preachiness is less unbearable than his jokes.

The portly man took a long puff on his cigar. That came from having been cracked, like a shank, once too often. Crushed like a pack of cards in a soldier's kit. The bayonet at his shin. His reflection in a warm gully.

—I said only it didn't sound too awful. What was the way of wisdom in that land? Not to be too smart about it. Considering the unpleasantness deposited regularly on the computer screen.

Words themselves had become clots of half-digested chime, bits of flesh and skin, lumps of pale, uncooked organs, speckled with blood. The sheer vileness of these creatures had never been quite so palpable. When the whole thing collapses (the old man sitting next to him said), as it will, no doubt about it, later in the century, the earth will give a vast sigh of relief, creating gales that make the mountains cross the continents like great slow yachts.

It had come at a price, but now at last the abused globe began the long, painful but always hopeful, process of recovery, it would take centuries, hell, millennia. Even though it had lost the species for which the words "abused," "painful," "hopeful," and "recovery" had a meaning. For which a word was more than a grunt accompanied by bad breath.

The wallet opened outward like a gesturing hand

or a beggar's smile. Crippled, lunatic and afraid of nothing. Like the code of Hammurabi painted on a grain of rice. The epidemic of laws and the nightmare of freedom, they said with twisted mouths.

—Perilously disposed? Not a bit of it.

At the bottom of the vat lay a crust of spider's eggs.

—Parachutes, tilburies, nasturtiums, hawthorn bushes, gear boxes, crankcases, peach blossoms, all lined up in what we thought was a speleological sequence. An archaeologist's botanizing spree in a technocrat's shirt pocket. I thought I heard them coming, but when I turned, they were gone.

—If only one can say it right once, one will not have to go on trying to say it forever. Between the burning bush and the pillar of fire. In retreat under the winter rain.

—Sasha . . . Sasha? . . .

—Yes?

—Where are you?

Silence.

—Where are you? . . .

—Nowhere.

Breaking icicles from the eaves, he had used them to write love letters to her in the snow. I couldn't guess who they were for, since no one else lived within miles. A few birds that remained through the season fled through the trees, the gray, spindly branches like ironic kanji grinning as the night fell.

The sun closed its third eye, and the moon edged up the eastern wall like the other end of an immense teeter-totter.

The swing swung slowly to a halt. And most of the children went home.

—I stayed, said Sasha. There was something about an empty playground in the evening, after everyone had gone home, that I always enjoyed when I was a child. I'm not sure why.

—I was harrowed when young by the photographs. They haunted my dreams that February and March, into spring, the skeletal bodies, the rags, the big, starving eyes. The terrible wheelbarrow. Of what order of evil was a man that he could do such a thing? If one person could, any person could, in theory. I myself could, given the right, the wrong, links in a monstrous chain.

—Spectres.

He felt his heart almost break. He must not think about it, but he could not help thinking about it. It opened a door to a hole of darkness, a door he could not close. No. Close but not quite lock.

—Because, as he said to her, any person could, in theory. One step into the pool only to step out again. However black the ink. What is this ungainly creature, a man? A human being? A woman? A man? A pool of darkness. What does science have to say about that? Nothing. Or rather, too much. It leaves you gasping for the air it has deprived you of even as it shears off your wings. The screaming babble of the internet. Which nothing calmed. Once. Twice. Ten thousand times. The nattering drill. At the heart of the light a black clot of blood. Embolism. The heart hammering with anger and fear.

—What you call a "pool of darkness," Sasha had said, in her patient, maddening repeater way. The attempt to peel off the scab merely reopened the wound. Somewhere deep beneath the scar. An umbrella furled like an intention. A quick walk across the plaza in the rain. The mercurial stabs at statuary bronzed to a deep blue-green, a verdigris you could

MEDITATIONS ON LOVE & CATASTROPHE AT THE LIARS' CAFE

almost smell. In that long-lost Italian spring. . . .

—Wake up, wake up, no, no, go back to sleep.

—Distant thunder in an Alpine sky, clouds piled up like a Louis Quinze wig, gamboling wings from the rookeries in synchronized cloudlike shapes above the city. The way the fog disappeared, crumpled like an old cornet and blowing like blazes above the fields across the river. You don't believe me? Neither do I, but that's what they said when all was said and done, don't go there even if your life depends on it.

A scrimmage of bumble bees in a jasmine bush.

A pinch of honeysuckle and the honey bleeds on the stamen as you pull it from the bottom of the stamen.

—Dina Fiore, whom I should have had a crush on at the time, he said, and didn't know I actually did until twenty years later.

—Ping! said Sasha, flipping a finger against his shoulder.

Wake up, wake up, no, go back to sleep. The dawn is still miles away. It's coming like a thief in the night.

—You still don't believe me?

The time of Pentecost had passed. The farmlands extended to the forest covering the hills like a lambskin glove. Perpetually bleeding in sorrow . . . .

. . . for our sins.

Sasha's eyes were a distant storm.

—Why can't you be kind?

—Gentleness is a heaviness, imagine carrying a toothpick in the palm of your hand, well, so, now imagine carrying it for a thousand miles. Anger, on the contrary, feels wonderful. You feel strong when you rage, ever notice that? Especially the righteous kind. Then you laugh afterward and everything is fine again. Amazing. But being sweet, gentle all the time—not on your life. I'd rather cry my eyes out. I have cried. I do cry regularly and on cue. Like a bloody, damned fountain. Weeping like a grove of willows by a long summer river. Weeping for the living, who have nowhere else to turn. The tears collected in small glass vials, then sealed and labeled 1347 or 1620 or 1896 or 2018. They gleam in the light and magnify the hand that holds them. You can even count the whorls on your fingertip. Here. Look.

—So I'll ask you again: why can't you be kind?

—There was a time I forfeited any hope for eternity, with a Moor grinning in a glass case and the cook laughing in the pantry. Grooms in the stables. A jockey in the mews. A fast pitch over the plate. And steroids that corrupted the game pretty permanently. Or till they become common as caffeine. The new normal on the drought-ravaged plains.

—It'll be without, he then said, rising to a shout, us. Sometimes only hysteria is appropriate.

She seemed to find his calm offensive, as though the thought of drowning made him sing inside. A landsman, this knight of the winged glasses. Uplifted, the rambling cars. Toward whatever outlasts the celebratory toasts and the spilled seed between the sheets.

—Another, please. I'm thirsty today.

The gonads are itchy and the drawbridge is out.

—Come quick, my nymphs! I want to worship your smooth, soft tummy, to taste the sweetness of your thighs. Your breasts are my clouds. Your face is the face of the goddess peering down at me in graciousness and pity. I kneel and pray in the forest of the delta I disappear in, such joy is your sweet crown. Let's drink the champagne of love, let's get drunk on each other's desire.

And the angels opened their wings and filled the sky (it expanded like a bubble) with snow.

—Give me another. Did I ever tell you about her? I shouldn't but I will. She never really flirted with—well! But that's the way it was then. The feminist rage of the hour. The wartime footing. The warrior's zeal. Bring 'em on.

The glint in her eye. Envy, pride, a lasting wreck. Miserable, but perfect. Even though the die hadn't yet been cast.

—The world was on the verge of bankruptcy,

yet I didn't even break into a sweat. Amazing how you can kid yourself that nothing is really wrong. The dim cowering into dimness. The ugly baldy's aggressive smile. The liter, or was it a kilo, of really bad coke.

—The problem is I simply couldn't stand you at times. But I'm helpless when you ask me for help.

—Only bearable when beautiful, I say, though maybe the better word is fresh. As in fish. Of course, you're not supposed to say so out loud. They'll tar and feather you and run you out on a rail.

The grocer's greeting. The cop's hand. The face gone suddenly sour.

—But why do you hate me so?

—Why should I like you?

—You have a point there. One must learn to smile despite the shrapnel in the groin.

He hobbled to the threshold of the bar and stared outside. A herd of gazelles leapt across the tall, withered grasslands. One at a time, then in a great mass, like birds.

Then she was gone.

The dim cowering into dimness, the young student of astrobiology was looking hopefully through the latest reports from Chile. Supernova, the results from CERN, a smear from Hubble, neutrinos faster than light, or so reported, and the discovery a few years ago of Higg's boson, the "God particle," because of which there are lumps of matter aggregating into stardust, a favorite team, and your crazy uncle in the time-space continuum. Without Higg's, the universe would be nothing more than a kind of infinitely expanding spritz.

—Like your crazy uncle, in fact. Everybody was talking about it, above all non-scientific types like him. It gave him a certain weight. It brought her down to earth. It brought them together with a bang. And voila: the Crab Nebula, quarks, protons and amino acids, amoebae, butterflies, panthers, doves, and the perfect proportions of Sasha's face.

She turned sharply to him and recalled, in a flash, the solemnity of their first encounters. It would have been intellectual to a fault had there not also been a spark of desire or was it merely curiosity, like the static in a comb in February. Setting off a shower of falling stars from the falling waters of her hair. For him she had been part body, part mind; she could see that clearly enough. The mind interfered with the body, the body interfered with the mind. The confusion robbed him of his ability to talk, and he babbled to the ceiling till morning in an unknown tongue. His heart was full of pity (always a stronger motivator than lust), for she was, after all, mad as a hatter and danced all night in his bed, wild as a wounded swan.

She turned sharply to him.

—Do not forget where you are, in a garden where dragonflies weave their way across the just opening roses, their heads in crushed, pink crowds. Hiking up the boulevards to a distant krak of mountains, our exquisite china balanced on the back of a stallion, we march to the end of the sandlot and present arms to a glassful of sunlight.

The withing knots. The expended edge. The unaccounted-for expense sheet in question. A pale tide. A crown of swords.

She had eyed him at first with interest but also suspicion. Would he be able to carry the eggs? To the top flight of the ever-expanding tower? It was a reasonable question though a little disillusioning. Not as excitingly mysterious as romantic love used to be. In a long lost generation. But then all explanations were disheartening—it was how you could tell they were true. They left not a rack behind or even a pitying smile, just one more "you really were an idiot" to go down with the toad you swallowed for breakfast that morning. Reality can be such a jerk, don't you think? But don't.

Sasha never told him anything, so how could he know? Her smile was hard as rock candy. Pascal looked awful when he said that. Why are we here? Oh yes, to buy a lottery ticket.

—Sometimes it's better just to dream.

The pale tide. Remarkable for the coral formations

at the edge of the forgotten beach.

Not that he was entirely a slave to memory, it was more like indentured servitude for someone who had always been suspicious of the future. In the oiled lock and subtle key of the present instance. A Sherpa on the edge of the ascent. The wary but always grinning companion. The tent half buried in the snow. The sharp smell of the wind off the ice. The photographs scattered over the bedroom floor.

—You see, he saw them as revelations of some sort of ultimate attainment of being, held on the hook like an elusive fish, some deep-sea denizen hiding in a pocket of the Marianas Trench, the giant squid much talked about, never caught alive, what was no more than illusions of stillness in time's relentless gale.

—Though he may have been wrong, of course.

—Enough of them in one place created a really satisfying collection. One after another lined up like cards in solitaire. Between the plates and the jewelry case, the belvedere and the slumber party.

They fed off the silver in the ditch. Robbing the factory floor of several continents of inexpensive labor.

He said, as he poked a cookie into his mouth.

—There were no excuses for how much we really enjoyed ourselves, and yet we did, didn't we?

Somehow that sounded completely wrong. In the moral sense, of course.

—They're only human, after all, said Sasha, but they're still monsters.

—You mean, he responded, we are still monsters. Raining on us, golden and crude, an almost unbearable munificence. Imagine a storming herd of white elephants. The perfect servant of our wishes. Has become our perfect master. Like a bug swallowed whole in Aladdin's lamp.

He might have been wrong of course, he thought almost immediately: there were so many ways to be off target when cracking homespun glass. Bearing down on the clean formica. Folded like paper in a machine. Or leaving things out to melt. It tasted fine, but only once.

—You've noticed, haven't you, said Sasha, that novelty is no longer in fashion: everything has to be copied or, preferably, stolen.

—I carried a bucket of them from end to end of the village but had not a single taker. The prayers flew up on all sides and got tangled in bees.

—If only people could be good, she said, and follow my commands.

—If only the world could be good, he said, and follow my wishes!

It was only occasionally possible and perhaps never was the point. Otherwise God seemed unfathomably cruel, even if you didn't believe in him. As if he cared what I believe, thought Sasha. He hangs his cloak of darkness over the firefly galaxies as if they were the shoulders of a king. But to become a king is to have taken (Pascal thought) the first step on the road to humility. Tell your god that, when he comes calling (Sasha thought). There never was a name for it. I know.

The sound of tapping against an empty drum. Angel's tears. Falling stars. The smell of rosemary on the outdoor steps.

—If I could be good, he said. There's a photograph of a range of horses all looking east as if they had forgotten home. Quiet but not lost, comfortable in their homey way and needing nothing more for the moment. Though that was necessarily a temporary condition. Comfort, that is, needing nothing. Not even air. Liftoff as in a flying dream, which the Jungians, those killjoys, are particularly uninspiring about.

—He really could be a twerp, that fellow, Sasha said.

—I'll fly in any direction I want to, Pascal declared defiantly.

After a very brief pause, she shouted, Bravo! Let the light man rise!

Balloons filled the sky like bubbles in champagne. They moved in a bunch above the city like a crowd of kids flying with brightly colored backpacks between their little wings, it was the sweetest thing you ever saw, they looked alive as they drifted away in the distance, it was also curiously heartbreaking, there was not a cloud in the sky. I want to join you, can I, can I, I can't wait, I want so much to join you up there, it'll make me happy, I know it, can I, will you let me? I promise I won't be a bother, I won't make a sound, you'll never even know I am there.

—So he let her rise, did he?

—She thought so; anyway, she had endless patience with him. Remarkable for one so young. I guess she loved him and that is what love is. Though he could try the patience of a saint. And did. Regularly. With extreme prejudice. As though there was nothing easier in the world. Plangent. Obscurity. A Scottish snap. The tessitura of darkness being an extremely high and an extremely low pitch, with nothing at all in between.

—They swam together in the meadow pond despite her fear of tadpoles (stated) and his own fear (unstated) of water mocassins. Children are like that, when not shockingly cruel, they can have astonishingly good sense. The truth was sometimes so obvious, so why all these arguments over the burning grass and the ruined fountain in the garden? Couldn't they just swallow their bitterness and raise their hands like the eyes of so many dolphins and winnow the sea wind with the waves? In other words, get on with it? When in doubt, give up.

Society wants you to be slightly stupid, so don't give them the satisfaction. Hide under the bed, don't grow up. Be foolish and free. Eat cake whenever you can afford it. You'll get tired of it soon enough and want to do the right thing, out of curiosity if nothing else. Virtue won't make you happy. Not vice, not money, not love. Happiness makes you happy, then it bores you and you decide to try misery just for a change. Though escaping misery is not the snap that escaping happiness is. The gate crashed open and, in the dark entrance, his horns flashing in the lights from the passing traffic, the Minotaur stood, black and silent.

—Be careless and free: now, there's a motto I could aspire to. Just as long as it includes no commitment. But it always does, of course. Foolishness, with its way of slanting a course toward the future however delightedly we threw ourselves into the present. Tomorrow wrested the baby from its mother's arms. And tossed it into an awkward hour despite its rage and tears.

It made them weep where they stood on the plain between the burning villages. The smoke buried the sunrise and the flames licked the morning's cold arms.

—For every hour in the world was alive then; I remember, I was there. And the brain scientists can go hang. I don't want to know what it is I can never know. The taste of blood after the fight with Bobby. The whiskey brown of Mariana's eyes. The cascades of apples in the Millers' barn behind the black-boughed orchards. I don't just remember a memory of a memory, he thought. I remember Sasha. Dewpoint. Tree line. Vortex in Tornado Alley. Your hair in the wandering wind, he thought. Your words I could never trust, she thought. Their eyes locked in that long, awkward dance at the end of the year.

—I like that thing you found when we were talking about the book on mazes.

—Oh? You mean between the hedgerows of that funky English garden?

—Well, perhaps. I thought you preferred guava jelly with your muffin, the glories of Nutella, chipped beef, cherries jubilee, and dead baby, that sort of thing. The sliced wheat toast. The apricot spread. The currant jam. English things, British things. Your tea is now ready, milord, would you like the Assam or the Lapsang Suchong? I so love how you fondle your shoe. The things that make one feel so, oh I don't know, serenely above it all. But I would never have said that.

—I'll get back at you for this, he thought as he grinned, sage and savage as he always got when he knew he was getting too happy. And she saw it too.

—Well, perhaps. Perhaps they were, perhaps they weren't, some questions are better left unanswered.

Take this photograph for instance. I could swear they both look angry, but I was there, their eyes were both in the sun, just before and just after they were giggling over some private joke. I've never seen two people who looked so pleased with each other. And themselves. The bastards. The camera can be the most cunning of liars. By freezing a moment it tells all sorts of lies, don't you think? I thought my whole life was leading up to one perfect moment of absolute, authentic being, and there I would freeze until I eventually vanished in some vague, far-off, abstract thing called "death." All because of photographs. Well, partly, at least. I was very young at the time. It took me a long time to realize it was the photograph that was the illusion, which had created this illusion of a final reality that one became; everything before it, and after it, being not quite real. But no, that idea, which I so liked, was just one more toy to throw onto the bonfire with my dreams, the sweetest things, let's face it, in life, the facts being iffy at best. And often nasty. Ever think about that? But Sasha had already grown bored and was thinking about what color to paint her toenails, this was a fact she preferred to make as little iffy as possible, after all she did have some control over that, and she did not believe in bothering her head about things over which she had no control. She had read that once in Epictetus, a far smarter fellow, she decided, than Dr. Phil.

—No, Sasha Kamenev said primly after a moment of reflection. I haven't.

—All because of photographs (Pascal thought again, ignoring her, or perhaps not hearing), and other mirrors of someone else's dream. Which someone called, in those years, the brain's natural state. Unquiet grave. Paintings in the gallery downstairs. Books piled in columns on the floor around the desk. Music from the third room down the hall. Portamento, that slick trickery of the devil, a sanctimonious generation had pointed out. To say nothing of parallel fifths. And espressivo was somewhere between a black shirt and a Gestapo unit. Poor romanticism being made to carry the coals of hellfire for several decades. Till most of that was forgotten by the rappers, and the sanctimonious wept tears of blood. Which was irrelevant to him, since he sank into Bantock as into Bliss. The beauty of it was he could still do exactly as he pleased. And despise the taste of the rest, which after all is what taste means. Elitism can be such a consolation. After all, when choosing fruit at a store, one does not usually choose the rotting apple. On these matters they were agreed. If that is the fruit of democracy, then the hell with democracy! To say nothing of capitalism, the slave and vampire of the masses. That was maybe too easy. But maybe not. So they began to build their island of happiness surrounded by a sea of fog, for we must hide ourselves from them, Pascal thought. And we'll send signals that can be deciphered only by our friends and those like-minded to us, Sasha said in her practical way. Even if we know there are no guarantees, and there may be no one out there like us. In that unquiet grave.

The stillness between the candle and its flame. Hollowed out like a decaying tree. Or a folded handkerchief in a mirror. Escaping eyes. The prevailing winds. A hypnotic torpor. The grandness of Pascal's many-pillowed sleep and how his dreams perpetuated the solemnity of that hour. As we waited, impatient and stern, for the brass gong to sound between the gleaming portals. Only words, Pascal complained. But such words, Sasha rejoiced. Keep tossing them and one or two are bound to stick. And then, eureka! A crack of light as the great locked gate soundlessly opens.

The prevailing winds. From east over the Atlantic. Across the gray, clammy tides, the puling seagulls, their black caps and flexing, sickle-like wings, the terns' small, quick arcs, the funny rushes and escapes along the skirt of the wave wash of the pipers hunting for small, nutlike sandcrabs. The acid briny scent, the yellow, impetigo-infecting gullies slick with scum. The gray white sand grainy with tiny white and black crystals he could almost count as they separated in his palm. Clumps of salt grass covering the dunes like long green hair. The endless distant roll and crash of waves along the beach, the lulling confusion of whiteness, a serene and tranquil drama raving and collapsing without a pause from horizon to horizon, of the shore.

When they met shyly in their swimsuits, the summer Pascal was sixteen and Sasha fifteen, and their families spread their beach blankets and chairs and umbrellas under the tinkling shouts and laughter of swimmers and beachball players and sandbucket diggers and sandcastle builders not far from the lifeguard stand on the hot white sand and the cool gray sand along the edge of the playful lashing mindless dazzling beautiful and frightening sea.

—No. Ocean. There is something grander in the word, don't you think? said the portly man, disturbing his daydream.

An unfathomable calm under the skittering nervousness of that day.

If he remembers. Well, not all that much, not really. It came and went in patches. Whirligigs and wormholes. Night vision and the wastage of armies. Green shadows. A whiff of fireworks scratching the face of a small, dark sky. A blithe heart, nevertheless.

In the fall, the wheatfields behind the porch and the restless glancing avenues, mock peevish and running away as fast as they could. Free as they could be. Racing the dust at their heels and shouting whoopee! Looking for love in the usual inept ways, and if not love, more money. A lot more money. Because it would have to do. And turned out to be considerably easier. It's the one thing one could actually get —easier than love, certainly, easier than justice, or truth, or beauty, or the good. Look at the stuff they could buy. The plunder, the stash and the loot. And they didn't even have to kill to get them. Did they?

—I don't know, did we? he said out loud.

And Aeolus filled their sails as the ship surged out of the harbor's embrace. White clouds.

—I'm sorry, old boy, did you say something? said the portly man.

—No, sorry, he said, flustered. I …

—A *lot* more money, someone said passing with a nod and two boots of Blue Moon.

—Creative destruction? Sasha had said then. So what happens when the creative gets disappeared, muchacho? Then all you've got is the destruction. Kind of compulsively destroying while waiting for the creative to get off its butt, and so you just keep on keepin' on, destroying, hell, it used to work man, it gotta work, it always worked before, until you've destroyed, well, just about everything. And you waiting there, like Didi and Gogo, for the creative bit to kick in.

Satan sits there laughing to beat hell, weeping with laughter, you idiots, he shrieks, he howls, he slaps his sides, you morons, he shouts, gotta love 'em, they've done all my work for me, Hitler failed, Stalin failed, Mao failed, Idi Amin failed, Pol Pot failed, who'd a-thunk my best buddy would be Adam Smith, Friedrich von Hayek and Milton Friedman! Hey, I'm down here! Right, come on down! The water's warm! In fact, it'll scorch your little buns off! Ha, ha, haah! Gosh, I adore you guys!

—It doesn't anymore.

Right. Not then and not now, he thought. Despite the multifarious extravaganzas, the impossible tasks written out on innumerable blackboards from end to end of the vast classroom, doing his sums under the torrid eyes of Mrs. Skinner and the academic elite who despised him.

—It doesn't get any better than this despite all your dreaming. Hope is its own reward as long as you don't entirely believe in it, otherwise you are one of the truly cursed.

—An entire relationship can subsist, she said one day, on good manners alone, though some people seem to think that passion . . . well.

—Bad boys excite the ladies.

—All that resentment's a challenge. Nice, juicy!

—And self-destruction's hot.

—Consider yourself lucky to have grown so wise so young.

—Lose your youth, lose your beauty, but never lose your manners. Yep: it sounds idiotic.

—Because, as you just said, she said, pointedly, hope is its own reward. Something like dreaming. An endless delay before awakening. As in Tantric sex.

—So they tell me.

She stared at him for a long moment.

—Stop me if you've heard this before, she

continued, in a mocking tone. The autonomous person cares principally about her own approval. Celebrity, fame are violations of privacy. Money and power are only useful for making real her fantasies. Love is sometimes pleasant, sometimes burdensome, always a distraction. Otherwise she'd be content to live in a cave on fresh bread and spring water.

—Doesn't she love anyone?

—Humanity is a lesson to be learned, an instrument to be used or an obstacle to be overcome. She doesn't waste her time worrying about humanity, unless she chooses to make their welfare a source of her own amusement.

—She sounds awful.

—Uberbitch, that's her! Sometimes she chooses compassion, even love—after all, they're a challenge, and one more conquest for her pride—but she'll be damned if she'll be blackmailed into them. She constantly reminds herself that her own strength is a fragile shelter, that everyone begins and ends weak, dependent and helpless. And that the dead are the most helpless of all.

—Does she despise weakness? Or only fear it?

—Both, but only in her more foolish moments. The question is, will she recognize the goodness that weakness makes possible—tenderness, sympathy, delicacy, grace, the openness to experience that the muscle-bound loses in its balled fist? Will she see in the weak what she once was and will be again, when old age, illness—mortality—beat her in the fight, and ensure her future will depend on others for all time to come?

—Or at least all of history. And when that wears out . . . well, we'll worry about that when it happens.

—So don't be too arrogant, guy! Got it?

She winked.

—So they tell me. In mocking and adventitious tones, before being crushed between an amino acid and a peptide, like some nervous clone. But don't wait too long for it. It has that strange mark of irony in the middle of its paw, did you notice?

—Not yet. Maybe later. Maybe never.

He kissed her gently on the nose.

—Get *out* of here!

Among the mountains of salt and the mines of Utah and Comstock. An unrelieved perplexity mounted on a throne. Throwing glances in a perspective of long, curved, shadowy halls. Their worried and aggrieved looks. Painful gestures beneath a towering clock. Close to bedtime and the journey's end. If you believe in the hour yet to come. Gin and tonics from his parents' era, fashionable again two generations later, in tall sweating glasses held in outstretched fingers. Pillowcases left hanging on the bannister. Arpeggios dancing lightly in the piano room.

—But I thought you loved music, said Sasha. Was I wrong again? Even though it was more like just banging notes, waiting for harmony, sweet harmony, to unveil her losses to the world. You said so. I distinctly remember.

That was the day before she ported the bureau without help to the top of the stairs and pushed. What an alarm of rocking, clattering, smashing, shattering overturning of secret drawers and perfectly folded underthings went flying, tossed and turning, as it lumbered end over end down that long far-flung flinging flight of stairs! It was quite rejuvenating though only a once-in-a-lifetime happenstance. And she felt so much better afterward—her eyes were sparkling for hours. She brushed her hands with a flush of satisfaction and went back to her room looking for something else to smash but alas there were only the bed and the vanity and they were too close to her heart to wreck however beautifully. So she took the old hat she hadn't worn in ages and threw it out the window, and it sailed off, spinning gently, across the yard and landed in the branches of the apple tree that was just beginning to blossom, it was the middle of May a very, very long time ago. And there it sat all summer in the sun and the heat and the rain and the night until the blackbirds slowly tore it to pieces and used the pieces to build their nests and the ants took off bits to their colony near the tulips and squirrels took other bits, no doubt thinking they just might be nuts, and the rain and weather rotted the rest. But by then she had forgotten all about it. She had been severely punished for the bureau toss anyway, but she found she didn't care.

—After all, Sasha felt so much better afterward. As Pascal did too, when he imagined a really big blow-up, dynamiting a city, say, or icing half Russia with a hose of ICBMs (he grew up during the Cold War). Though today he might be piloting a drone over Raqqa or sweeping across the hills of Yemen where he sat at his desk in Idaho, his palms sweating in the air-conditioning and his conscience raging at him for not really caring that the SUV he just blew up was probably carrying a young couple to a family reunion or a bunch of young men drunk on illicit beer, the target having lost his cellphone with the GPS code under the back seat next to a dirty keffiyeh and an empty bottle of Dr. Pepper. It lacked a certain heroism. And he imagined how he would be hated in the future, the faceless killer from the sky, he and his countrymen, his country. And how that hatred, like seeds, would grow into a jungle nobody could cut through. At the end of the grotesque civilization he called his own. This was his mantra for a season. There is no justice, there is only revenge, and it is only a matter of time before they will bring their revenge home. Because his dreams were no longer only dreams. They instantly oozed into reality and froze there, shining icicles surrounding his head like a crown.

—Yes, said Sasha after hearing him out. It does lack a certain heroism.

Though you never know, he thought, what might be happening elsewhere, at another time, in another place. In the land of perhaps, the Cockaigne of possibility, far from the desert of must and will. A lake beneath a patient, murderous drone. Compact with futurity and the august, prehensile tail of a maleficent dragon. The stinking rage of combat.

—To say nothing of the missed purgatory of home, he thought he heard someone saying down the bar. His back was turned to him, so the words were not entirely clear. The portly man was silently discussing a pint of ale.

—Though this purgatory sent you down from paradise, the back went on, as you awaited the end of the long penance for having been so happy and the reward at last of a secure place in hell. Called adulthood, if I remember correctly, said the back, Pascal could see the back's hand holding a glass half-full of whiskey and a single cube of ice. Pascal nodded, as if in agreement, at his own reflection in the mirror just past the bartender's waist.

The song of the ocean was noisy in his ear, and the sky turned violet with sunset.

—She never did return my heart, you know, someone else seemed to be saying, close to his shoulder, leaning forward conspiratorially, as if into his ear, so I walk around with a hole in the middle of my chest. Like the messy end of a shotgun blast. I can hear the wind whistling through me as I walk the city streets late at night.

One might have lived a virgin for all that, Pascal thought wistfully. Sex was so much more beautiful in fantasy than in reality.

The unpleasant odor of it, for one thing. And its paradoxical combination of predictability and unde-pendability. To say nothing of the emotional com-plications that always ensued. The guilt, since sex for Pascal always involved hurting someone's trust: there never seemed to be sex without betrayal. So that the only honorable thing to do was to have sex with no one. Or only with oneself.

It just seemed to be another part of the ordeal of civility. Yes, that may have been sex's dirty little secret.

—Sex is a chore, the portly man sighed, as if reading Pascal's thoughts. It is like eating the same dessert every night for the rest of your life. It's nauseating, in the end, and attempts to vary it, to make it always new and exciting, are hopeless and futile. The promisers of the sexual millennium were charlatans and liars. He took a final swig of his mug before saying, with a walrusy groan, Though how one wanted to believe them!

The only time Pascal's sex life was really bad was when he was in a "relationship," when he suspended his solo activities in deference to his girlfriend, who, whoever she was, never had sex with him as often as he was used to having it with himself. In his early youth he had DIY sex at least once or twice a day. An orgasm a day keeps the shrink away, was his mantra. Now, no sane girlfriend would let that happen past the "honeymoon"; if she did, it was invariably a sign she was a lunatic. In Pascal's limited experience, only crazy ladies and female neophytes enjoyed sex. Sane women, once their curiosity was satisfied (which usually happened by the end of the first night), put up with it to please their men or to have kids. This was the theory he had never discussed with Sasha.

—Well, the inevitable breakup was usually a huge relief, said a fellow in the bar who had known Pascal since he was a kid. No female ambiguities, no ambivalences, no mood swings, no clashing emotional claims, and he could have as much sex as he wanted on his own terms and on his own schedule. Free at last!

—He liked women well enough, said a tall, square-shouldered guy with orange hair who had

also known Pascal a long tine, but he told me he'd
rather face a prison term than have to be married to
one. So the decision to make all of his relationships
platonic was easy, especially when he discovered internet porn, that sexual paradise: six different girls
a day if he wanted (which he never actually did, but
how nice to have the option), and no whining, arguments, bad moods or nasty comments. He told me it
was part of his secret recipe for being content with
life in a world that was, or at least seemed on the surface to be, mindless, soulless and heartless. He once
said, "I built an iron wall around my soul, and only
regretted it when the fantasy, the idea and hope, of
true and deep and abiding love for and by a woman
of my own choosing, overcame, as strong fantasies
will, my better judgment."

—The bastard told me he admired virgins, a
third man chimed in, ruefully, holding a pint of por-
ter in a grubby paw. They'd avoided falling into the
trap. They had beautiful daydreams about love. They
longed for it. "That longing," he told me, "those
daydreams, were the most intense happiness I ever
knew. Reality is envious of happiness, and therefore
kills it. Virginity keeps you happy while frustration
tortures you, because you never stop believing."

Innocence and hope. Knowledge is a dead end.
The curse of innocence is its belief in knowledge.

Sometimes he missed having sex with a woman,

but it passed when he remembered the price (enormous) that every woman had exacted from him after he slept with her, the awful hangover after the splendid, all-night spree.

—To be free at last, someone nearby sighed.

—But that might require a more radical solution, the first fellow said. A leap into more or less of a void. A rope. A razor. A pill. A pistol. A bridge. A belt. A plastic bag. A car in a garage. A gas oven. An escape. A mad dash for the exit.

—Then the idea came to him more and more often. It was comforting.

—The great compensations of love and art had proven hollow. Neither men nor women were for him, and he wasn't for them. His paintings were most useful as sheets during winter. His artistic pretensions had earned him more contempt than admiration or affection. He'd failed almost completely.

—Not quite completely. He had a few admirers.

—Two brain-damaged young men who kept calling him a genius in shell-shocked tones and an ugly fat old woman who drooled whenever she saw him and propositioned him once a year; these were the result of several decades of pursuit of love and fame.

—His self-contempt almost strangled him, since he really had nobody else to blame. Suicide would have been a blessing, but he lacked the courage and character for that. And so he lived, hating himself, hating God for creating him and then denying him the only things he had ever wanted, hating life for the deep fraud he felt it was. Life, he thought, was a deception of matter, matter pretending to be spiritual, and humanity, with its accomplishments, civilization, culture, etc., was the most highly developed example of that fraud.

—Curiously, the idea that life was a deception, from the tiny prisons of its cells to its most complex incarnation in human civilization, gave him a feeling of victory, a kind of calm.

—You're a liar, he said to the day. You're a liar, he said to the sun. You're all liars, he said to stars, roses, women, streets. You tempted me to hope, but there's nothing to hope for beyond the air in my lungs, the bread in my mouth, the sounds in my ears, the light in my eyes. And they are not enough. And so, he said, with a profound sense of relief, may my curse be upon all of you.

But he lacked the courage and character for that.

It was almost too demeaning, Sasha thought. To be hampered in that way despite all the options at the time. The seeming options, anyway. Because once you've done something, it seems as though it had always been meant to be, and so maybe the options were illusory after all. Amor fati . . .

—If only!

—No, really. Plus the beauty of matter, in Joubert's lovely phrase. Because he was right, that Frenchman with the shy ambition and the small, beautiful notebook. So beautiful in its bold modesty, its humble bravado. All that clean, beautiful white space surrounding the few lovely words. No overwrought romantic windbaggery for him. (Sasha caughed discreetly!) But I'm drifting from the subject. Though what indeed was the subject? She looked at him with her usual skepticism. Did she love him? Maybe she did, in her peculiar way. They had not yet slept together or even as much as kissed. But that meant nothing. He was actually more afraid of it at forty than at sixteen. He had decided to kill himself if a woman broke his heart again. This will keep you chaste better than a hellfire sermon.

—He thought the worst thing ever to happen to him was feminism. It had been good for the women, yes, he could see that, but it had turned his life into a little corner of hell.

—But then, all life is hell, he told her one day. Calmly, matter-of-factly. I wish I could say I love it. I wish I could say I love you.

—Me too.

Then they parted for three days. Three weeks. Three months. Years. Decades. But not forever. They were adults. You would have thought they had learned never to be entirely sincere, that was what always got young people into so much trouble, their infatuation with sincerity, "honesty," no relationship will last five minutes of complete *that*.

—No, apparently not.

—And so they tormented one another with their precious truth. You are my hell. A Sartrean proverb! And no one can leave hell. You see the problem.

But that meant nothing. Never even turned a hair. Minimally extant as it was. The withers unwrung, the moist appeal in the gathered vats, the wayward affront. The absolute right to happiness and to one's own life. The boy on the hill came to that conclusion one afternoon in the fall, as he was walking through the tall, yellowed hay at the edge of the field that bordered his family's property. It was startlingly true. No one had the right to deprive him of his happiness, wherever and however he found it. No one had the right to force him to sacrifice his happiness to anyone else, to a group, society, country, army, religion, company, class. They might have the power, the strength, even have the legal right, but they did not and could not have the moral right. And in that discovery lay his strength. His right to happiness was absolute; this would become his moral compass: *my happiness is my good.*

No, it didn't turn the fellow into a monster. First, he readily acknowledged the mutuality of his insight: that, just as no one had the right to deprive him of happiness, he had no right to deprive others of happiness either. This seemed logical, right and natural. He also soon saw that the happiness of others increased his own, and that the biggest threat to his happiness was other people's pain: the greatest source of happiness even at the core of its pain was love, and not love for one but love for all. Life was happiness before it was pain.

—Or was it the other way around? No matter.

Pain is useful as a warning, and is one of the prices of love; but suffering, which is pain beyond any value as a warning or as love's price, and, when suffering becomes a part of love, it is a sign of a sickness, of the failure of love. Suffering in itself has no value; it is the face of evil. Pleasure is the meaning of goodness; the one exception being forms of pleasure that do others harm—the goodness of such pleasure is canceled out by the injury it causes. The good life is a life of constantly varying pleasures that cause no harm. Art is a clever means by which we turn even the world's greatest evils into pleasure: aesthetic satisfaction.

—Even Auschwitz?

—*Even Auschwitz*. Some might consider this immoral; on the contrary, it is one of the purposes of human life.

—And what are the purposes of human life,

Herr Professor? What is its meaning?

—The meaning of human life is to know truth, to create goodness and beauty and overcome ugliness and evil, to share love, and to enjoy existence; to turn evil into *good*, however modest; simply by providing comfort to someone who is suffering, for example. Your will can transform any evil into good.

—Even the spectres?

—What do you think? But to do so takes intelligence, talent, sensitivity, knowledge—above all: *will*. This is called the triumph of the human spirit, and it is our connection to ultimacy, to transcendence, to the gods. This frightens, even disgusts some people, but it shouldn't. It is one of our most powerful tools in subduing the human condition to our will and our will to the divine. It is one of man's highest purposes, a spiritual form of medicine as well as of discipline. The tragic artist is a kind of surgeon of the soul: he cuts through intellect and bone and flesh to the heart, in order to save it. The blood on our hands is the blood of our salvation. Our salvation is in our hands; the gods will help us, but first we must act. Our actions please them, and they descend and raise hymns of honor at our death.

This he thought with a furious thought, and he took it to his love with a tender sweetness. Knowing this, he said, makes even death a source of joy, the much-wanted sleep at the end of a strenuous, exhausting, harrowing, and, if we look at it in the right way, thrilling life. But it is up to us to *make* the thrill, he told her excitedly, with our hearts and hands and brains. And she listened to him with shimmering eyes.

—For life is happiness before it is pain.

—Or is it the other way around?

—Ah yes, an instrumentality unrecognized in its time. Well begun being half done. And other hopeful folklorisms.

—The smell of paint and turpentine, he said nostalgically. How it lingered in the house for days. The smell of the new. So many such novelties we were granted, it opened the porch to the sweet-briny tartness of late spring morning in farm country. There, just like that, and it brings it all back. The sunny rooster's cockcrow and the odor of the chicken coop, it made all your senses dance, keen with morning. The distant chuff and groan of a tractor in a field still all mud and thick, overturned clay. The fluttery opening of the snapdragons and the tiny bluebells and the unfurling dogwood and the flickering of robins and swallows and red-winged blackbirds through the trees' dappled leaves. The smell of the future was in the air. All promise, all hope. I was glad, intensely glad, to be alive. At times I felt so happy I almost cried. My parents seemed to be so much in love, and their love filled our household with cheerfulness and laughter, and I so looked forward to growing up if that meant being like them. What happened, he cried out in despair, when did I lose that promise, that hope, when did I learn to believe it had been a lie, all of it?

—But it wasn't a lie, she said patiently. Then angrily. It was never a lie. It changed. The earth rolled over in its bed of night, and the world heaved a long sigh under the moon, and woke under another sun. But don't shame your youth. Whatever was forever is. Whatever was forever will be. Whatever was is forever.

His silence wanted to believe.

—Yes, the smell of the future was in the air. There was indeed no greater happiness than hope. Fulfillments disappointed always. Love, fame, wealth, all hope and nothing fulfilled, every one of them had been, whether denied or, even more bitterly, fulfilled, tawdry, mocking. As though he were being punished. Though for what crime he had not been told. Perhaps hope itself, with all its sweetness, was the curse.

He worked hard, burnt the midnight oil, rose with the cows, kept himself informed, humbly memorized what his masters bludgeoned into his skull. What hobbled him was his scorn for the society he lived in. As he grew older, he came to suspect the flaw was not in his society but in society itself, in humankind, humanity, himself, in existence, a crack in the heart of being. Men and women were shabby, flawed, shameless, in their essence. In their genes. Darwinian selection had winnowed out certain forms of goodness as maladaptive, and winnowed in certain forms of evil, as helpful for survival, that most necessary, most questionable, of values. Though, many people were not even evil, they were merely like damaged fruit, that hated anything not itself, that it could not share, because it made them ashamed, and this they could not bear once they had escaped childhood, though in a sense no one ever escapes childhood, adulthood being a kind of mutual agreement not to call each other's bluff: "adults" forming a kind of society for the preservation of mutual self-deception. Often lazy or brutal or stupid, they (we, he thought) sought to destroy, or at least dismiss, what they (we) did not understand. And so one day you decided to turn your back on society and cultivate your own happiness by creating beautiful objects and telling yourself bitter and bracing truths. And collecting a few agreeable, supportive if not uncritical, mutually appreciative allies, thus *creating your own minority* who would keep each other laughing and warm, exhilarated and encouraged, against the iciness of reality and the indifference and brutality of some many of your fellow human beings.

Eventually he ceased despising humanity and

learned to pity them. He looked at people as people look at animals in a zoo. Tend to look, because some people look at such animals they way they look at people in society. With a kind of appalled pity. A pity that became an odd source of contentment. He even learned to love them again, once he stopped expecting anything from them and got over his excessive self-pity. He recognized their weaknesses in himself. And he pulled himself down from the pedestal he had unwittingly placed himself upon. This discovery was at first humiliating, then he realized that even his sense of humiliation was only another expression of his own arrogance.

And he burned with shame.

Sometime later he became a little more forgiving, grudgingly, of his fellows and of himself.

In the fullness of time, he became a small saint or wise man whom the locals visited with their problems, admiring, even loving him. And this came as the greatest surprise of all. Men and women are indeed not entirely worthless, he thought. *Pace* Sigmund, who notoriously claimed they were. And he turned to a woman he loved in secret, who loved him also in secret (they were both too afraid to tell their love to each other and so suffered and joyed entirely in their imaginations and were never disappointed by reality), and said, Maybe humanity is not absolutely awful, if they can love someone as worthless as myself, then maybe there is hope for us all.

—Maybe there is, she said with an ironic look. But then you haven't been crucified. Yet.

—No, he said, laughing lightly.

Then he looked as though he had just remembered something.

—Loving them is *hard*.

—Yes, she said. I know.

Pity became an odd source of contentment. Perhaps that was inevitable. Many had thought it might lead eventually to a really grand gesture, though others were not terribly disappointed when it didn't. Because they knew where grand gestures can take you. Gulags. Buchenwalds. Computer factories in Xanshi. Raqqas. Something aching at the back of the mind. The tang and foretaste of a really grand failure. Though you were always allowed to try again. That is the essence of the attempt. If not of the inescapable follow-through. For that one may pay a distinctly heavy price. As long as a student loan and deep as the Mariana Trench. To the molten core. Where they burned.

—The foretaste. At the bottom of the sky, he looked up to see the newest of cloud formations. *Undulatus aspiratus.* It was like standing at the bottom of a lake and looking up to see frozen swells like a pod of great whales caught in a vast amber made, paradoxically, of azure.

—There is no catastrophe that doesn't create its peculiar beauty. This may be its justification, something to give the watching gods a thrill. Look how wars bear stories like trophies, and despised love songs and poems like so much sun-warmed fruit.

—The gods make us suffer so we'll make better music, he said. The more they whisper, the more they'll sing. Listen to the stories, read the poems, bask in the music, look at the magnificent pictures.

—Make them suffer so they'll make us laugh, clap, cry.

—There is nothing like a bed of fire to make them dance like gods.

—Don't spare the lash, brothers, sisters, don't be afraid of shame's deep sting. They'll thank us with grateful hosannas when they see what comes out. Hell is the price of admission to paradise, he said.

She shook her head in a kind of baffled assent. You're really a nut, she said.

—What else can I do? To be sane in this world is to be a lunatic indeed. And he repeated: The gods make us suffer so we'll make better music.

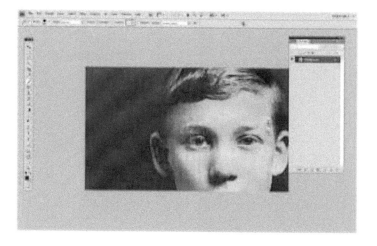

Incantation at the back of a small chapel. Where nuns lie, their arms spread cross-like, like dry leaves on the ground. Or wounded crows. The cantus firmus can be followed easily as each voice enters, an alto here, a bass there, a tenor there, then the sopranos again, until the entire chorus is singing in an aural brocade. The voices pause to allow other voices to sound, then, with cheerful wit, overlay and seem to try to hide the other voices, but never for long, and never successfully, as the voices underneath and behind make a brave showing, slowing down, speeding up, getting louder or softer, drawing attention to themselves, and the mind is both sharpened and dazzled by the layered, sweet complexity of sounds, the seemingly endless play of echoes. And you are surrounded and swept up in the rich yet strangely wistful beauty. A short spell of heaven. Or scratching the floor of paradise. From below, naturally. Then one at a time, the voices cease until only one is left, a high solo soprano softly fading away on a cadence, the last statement of the cantus firmus. And you are returned to the dusty light in the poorly maintained chapel. To the smell of boiling cabbage beneath that of dissipating incense. The dripping candle wax on the altar. The priest's nasal voice. The sore on your lip. Your foot, which is full of pins and needles from not moving for the last half hour. It was like a spell. And now you wake up. Or go back to sleep.

A spell of heaven. Inevitably short. For, after all, humanity cannot bear too much joy.

—I guess not, she replied. Though I wouldn't exactly mind being tested.

—As though they were not being tested. Did they even know how happy they were?

—Who does? We only know for sure the happiness we've lost, and only believe in the happiness we hope for. Silly human psychology: we're blind to the joy at our feet.

—The point of it? I'll give that up to the philosophers and poets, the theologians and priests of the new religions. The purpose of mine? To build a house for my joy so, if I ever find it, it has a place to sleep out of the night and the rain. What about you?

—Could I have a corner there to curl up in out of the weather? I'll be very quiet, you'll never even know I'm there, I'll just breathe the air of your little paradise.

He looked at her gravely.

—You're asking too little for yourself. It's not right.

—But it's all I want.

—My home will not be paradise. You give me too much credit. And power. I'm cold, and silent, and selfish. I only care about myself. I can't possibly . . .

—Please!

—I can't . . .

—Please! I'm kneeling here, praying to you. . . .

—Get up, get up, pray to your God, not me, I'm weak, harsh, I'm small . . .

—You are my heart's god.

He stared at her, appalled.

—This conversation never happened.

But it burned its flaming letters into their minds. Sometimes the words never forgotten were the ones not spoken.

—What about you? You left a photograph in the bathroom. It shows three cows and a separation, cyan, crimson, yellow, on the back of an old Pontiac a really gruesome dirty aquarium green. Not that he owes us anything, but there will be other birthdays.

—The cows that were there, whether we were or not.

—Excuse me?

—In our hovels!

—I thought I told you: I did believe in it. I just don't like parading things. But you can be as famous and rich as you like. I like successful people if they make their own breakfast. It shows they haven't forgotten where they come from. Eggs, bacon, grits and coffee. And the soil of Alabama. Wring it wet like seaweed over her forehead. Small curls, vivacious and cute. Always smiling. Except when not.

—Why are you being so literal-minded? Don't you know there is no such thing as exactly what I mean? And then there's all that poppycock about the void. And memes. And dissolving nanotechnology, left over from the '90s. That ancient time when the internet was just a toy. And not the web in which we are all caught like flies. And everyone is vying for the role of top spider. They're playing with fire, mark my words. The captains are gathering their drones in the abandoned Moffett field. Yemen was just a practice shoot. I think China will be a far more interesting target.

—But let's not ruin the party with talk of politics. The news is just too depressing. The ice caps are melting. North Korea has launched another rocket that could just reach California, bless it. Al-Qaeda is expanding across Africa. A wave of tornadoes struck the Midwest in the autumn for the first time in memory. And the new president . . . ! Etc. But I'm dating myself: by the time you read this you'll have disasters that make ours look tame. After all, if you're reading this, we survived whatever awfulness we went through; it's as stale as last year's newspaper.

—Except when not. When push comes to shove, you'll know it when you see it. The grail that came with the Meissen breakfast set. The little spear aligned with the crystal fork. The tiny robe folded like a napkin. The little bones the Roman soldiers were playing with. The tongs in the sugar bowl. When we were on a quest for the one certainty we ever knew. A bit of phenomenon from the old country placed tastefully in the living room and the remarkable turn at the bottom of the stairs. Into what can only be described as darkness.

—Hey! Hello down there! Is anybody home?

—This was in the early years before technology became so smart it was scary. When it guessed what you wanted before you even thought of it. When the servant, with a smile, became the master. And we groveled before this new king, god, mother, father.

—And I thought it wouldn't be so terrible. After all, how many doomsday prophets have been wrong over the last three millennia?

—One of them may get it right. Someday. It stands to reason. Though reason be damned.

—I was an idiot.

—Of course.

He looked at her wryly.

—You weren't supposed to agree.

—But I don't. I didn't. I can't.

The key turned with a thunk.

—Like a bit of phenomenon. From the old country. As opposed to the thing-in-itself, don't you know, forever unattainable, or just thing, the unattainable thing.

—Did you ever realize how divorce destroys in a particularly cruel way even the happiest memories of a marriage? How every memory of some joy you may have had is poisoned by the knowledge of what followed? How it makes you feel like a fool, humiliated, publicly mocked? As if the original harm had not been enough, but you must be made to pay for your hopeful faith, your stupidity, until the full term has been met? And you do not know what the full term will be until it has been met? It could be a lifetime. It is like the day you lost your faith in God, only now does it come home to you, you have lost your faith in pretty much everyone and everything. And for a time you fluctuate between despair and desperation until you learn that being terrified all the time will not save you, neither will obsessing, renewing the trauma over and over, save, even protect you, and at some point you grow a numbness like a callus over the stump of your mind, and learn to sleepwalk through much of the day, anything to avoid the scorching spasms that even now sometimes without warning shoot through you like electric fire. And even learn again, like the victim of a stroke relearning how to walk or speak, how to enjoy a fleeting moment of, yes, they used to call it pleasure. And finally open again the clenched white fist of your heart.

—You seem to be speaking from personal experience, she said.

He said nothing but turned toward the window where the dawn light was just beginning to outline the lazily flapping blind.

—Yes, it could be a lifetime.

—If love must be mutual to be real, then maybe he had never been in love, he said. Let's call him Joe. Joe had been on the receiving end of crushes, had suffered from infatuations, etc., etc., but never had it been mutual, at the same time and place. Though, given how love can wreck one's life, it may have been just as well he had missed it. Slowly—very slowly— it dawned on the never-too-quick-on-the-uptake Joe that he may have been happier this way after all. He had also never been struck by lightning, had never won the lottery or become famous or rich or powerful, all things much desired by some people that nevertheless often led to catastrophe. Like being struck by lightning. Or like winning the lottery. Maybe being protected from love was a blessing. Instead of falling in love with one person, Joe could love, in a less hyperventilating way, the entire world.

It had its own luxury. For example, Joe could live entirely for himself, his pleasure, his "interests." He would never have to share, never have to negotiate, bicker and fight over his time, attention, possessions, Joe would have a liberty, both internal and external, that (so long as he was prudent) no one would be able to take from him (anyway, in this life) and that many might envy, he could travel, stay at home, visit, keep to himself, rent an hour of physical love or go solo with his favorite porn stars without guilt or need for secrecy, he could be free in a way that a lover, and, a fortiori, a spouse, can never be. Joe could choose his virtue. And no one could stop him.

This was a delicious sensation.

Without love, Joe would have, in compensation, freedom, above all from other human beings. Love was a prison—or rather, love was the enticement, the bait, to enter the trap of human relations, the web of generation. And when Joe realized this, which is one of the deepest, most scandalous, most liberating truths about the human condition, his heart danced with joy.

—I can't honestly say I approve of that story, she said.

—That's because you're a woman, he said.

—That's sexist, she said sharply.

—Well—I am a chauvinist, yes I be, men should

run our fair count-ree . . . But no (he said thought-fully, pausing), I think the country should be run not by men and not by women and certainly not by me . . . just by those who stay out of my way, please, thank you, nice to have met you, now will you please run along and mind your own business, good-bye!

—She didn't leave Pascal, of course, because, in spite of everything—and he could be exasperating [Editor's Note: The rest of this chapter contains a certain amount of mansplaining, so some readers may want to skip to page 96]—she loved the fellow and was convinced that, by her example, she would one day change him. His mind. His heart. His DNA. His neurons (brain plasiticity being all the rage). Whatever. For he didn't realize, not for a long time to come, that renouncing love doesn't mean you escape it. Love had created him. Love owned him and might do with him what it would.

—And this was a delicious sensation too. What I shall now describe. All that time and sometime later. The feeling of . . .

—Well, what?

— . . . of doing absolutely nothing whatsoever.

—Nothing? Good luck with that!

—Well, as close to it as not actually dying. Lying in bed, staring at the ceiling as the shadows from the curtain moved across it, at the behest of the great turning earth under the magnificence of a hot, distant sun, watching without thinking or feeling or, for heavens' sake, willing, not reading or listening to music or watching television or surfing the internet or talking on the cellphone or planning or remembering. Vegetating. Sensing. Enjoying the blood as it moved through his veins. A curious peacefulness, a refusal of unease and worry. The world could go on without him for an hour, a day, a year, it could do quite well, thank you very much, and he could do what he had always wanted to do: live in pure contemplation, treating his life as a tourist treats a country he is visiting, gaping at the marvels, absorbing the atmosphere, observing the quaint customs of the colorful inhabitants, enjoying the bizarre fashions, the ingenious garments, the striking cuisine, the curious traditions, the beautiful architecture, the exquisite artworks, the marvelous music, the dramatic history, the fascinating stories, the sublime poetry, the majestic films, the thought-provoking drama, the profound philosophy, the delightful sense of humor, the mysterious beauty of the women, the audacity and cleverness of the men, the power of the religion, the messy but oddly effective economy, the messy but oddly ineffective politics, the astonishing balance of all the parts despite the inevitable conflicts, the murderous wars, the internecine strife, the ubiquitous crimes, the blood on the sidewalks, the shots in the dark, the laughter of the lunatics, the suicides of the druggies, the prostitution of body, mind and soul in the name of unrelenting greed, power hunger, sensuality, self-righteousness, self-absorption and self-importance inflating like a balloon to blank out a whole night of stars, and an absolute hatred of the weak, the old, the failures, the poor, but never to take part in it, this celestial festival and carnival of the gods, except as a well-disposed visitor, a kind and gentle fellow, a genuinely nice guy who wishes everybody well and nobody any harm whatsoever, on the contrary he loves to see people smile and so he wants everyone to be happy and nobody to suffer, but refusing to commit himself to a world that, after all, is not his own, that ultimately has nothing to do with him, no, they must iron out their differences, settle their disputes, clean the blood from their knives, destroy their weapons, abandon their bank accounts, their stock portfolios, their insurance policies, forget their belief in salvation, die or kill each other off from their mutual hatreds or not, and solve the dilemmas of their destiny on their own, as everyone must, as he must. Or perish in the attempt. Or rather, and perish in the attempt.

—I'm just passing through this world, he would often say. I'm in it, I'm not of it.

—Ah yes, said she. You are like a cereal box toy moving its tortuous way through the bowels of life.

—My world is elsewhere.

—In a cavernous cavity, gleaming pale and serene, swept with clean water and drained at its center to nether regions below of tunnels and caves out to the frolicsome, sunlit world above, after labyrinthine journeys through sewerland, cesspool and city chemical treatment plant.

— That's not quite it. The world is like a set of clothes you wear and change and ultimately discard. I enjoy it, then I pass it along to someone else. I even love much of it, as I love an old T-shirt. But it isn't mine, I don't own it, it doesn't belong to me, I don't belong to it. It's a castoff, pretty as a young woman's skin. It's something to use and love, then toss, as the world generates new shapes, forms, energies, things, beyond anything I can possibly dream up or possibly use. Maybe more than any of us can.

—He lived in the quaint faith that, in the baffling race of the human species, of all life, to self-destruction, the ineffable *it* would win.

—You mean, she said, that they would fail?

—Exactly. That they would survive—their genes, their memes—despite themselves.

—As I said, it was an ineffable faith. Which does not meant it was necessarily untrue, of course.

—Of course.

—After all, I have an ineffable faith in you. Don't tell me that means I'm wrong!

—Of course, she smiled, not.

—It just isn't my home. My home is elsewhere.

—Fine, great lost one, where is your home then? She often chided him on this idea of his. I always suspected that you, above all, were an alien.

—How could I know? But this place feels as far away from being a home as a place can possibly be. It reeks of hostility and cruelty under its benign but deceptive sun.

—You read that somewhere.

—I just made it up.

—Well, I wouldn't be so proud of it.

—Why not? he said. In this world I feel grudgingly tolerated at best. Sometimes I feel I'm on probation for a crime I can't remember committing. Have you ever had that feeling?

—Yes, she said thoughtfully, but I always felt it was because I was a woman.

—Don't fool yourself.

—Why not?

—Ah! That's what I always say! Male, female, hermaphrodite, transgendered, nongendered, sexuality unknown or nonexistent: none of that is relevant anyway. The crime is being born. If not crime, the extreme inconvenience, for all concerned: mother, father, family, government, universe, God. I, for example, was not extremely wanted. How could I have been? No one could have predicted who I would become. But that's not the point: the presence of anything leaping in the womb at that moment was disastrous for the couple in question. Anyway, I fit nothing here, and nothing here fits me. Natural selection! It's perverse. A psychopath, or sociopath, as they like to call it now, who knows why, they're always changing the words in the desperate hope they might thereby change the world. Heartless and mindless and soulless. Do you think the universe (he turned to her suddenly) might be fundamentally insane?

—It managed to create us, she said. Clever psycho!

—And yet might it have had something like a heart, mind, soul from the very beginning, if it was ever to be able to create them? In principle, so to speak. As "ideas," in a sense.

—At the beginning of the universe there was only energy, quarks, gas—there was no such thing as "liquid," it was too hot for anything to have "liquefied"—and yet today we are free to swim and surf in it, bathe and bubble in it, dash under a roof to escape its showers, get drunk from it and drown in it. So: did "liquidness" exist in principle from the very beginning of time, even before time? Would it exist in principle even if the universe had remained forever too hot or too cold to allow for "liquidness" of any kind? In principle, it must exist, must have always existed, must always exist in future, even when hell freezes over. Nothing comes from nothing, she concluded, primly.

—Maybe everything comes from nothing, he said. A warp in spacetime. A blip in the quantum vacuum. Or a breakout spore of antimatter from a neighboring, or the extra dimension of an overlaying, universe. Physicists these days are having crazy ideas. Maybe we're a piece of graffiti being signed on a brane by some druggy punk in a slum in a forgotten Third World city at the backend of a tenth-rate universe already half-decayed to nonbeing between entropy and its own version of dark energy.

—That's a cheerful thought, she said. In that case since our situation would seem to be entirely hopeless, we can relax and let the thing go to perdition in its own shabby-spectacular, peculiarly universal way.

—Ancient, exploded hypotheses, he said. But don't fool yourself, I tell myself, stupidly, because how can I even know? There's plenty of time. Or there's no time at all. There's always enough time. Or there's never enough time. If you start on time, will you end on time? If you start on time, I'll be surprised; if you end on time, I'll be shocked. One thing about them: they never arrive on time. They have no respect for time. Do you have the right time? Do you know what time it is? I just have no time at all. Why are they always late? Who are always late? Why, women, of course. But they aren't. But they are. Have you ever once known a woman to show up early for anything? (Pause for pondering.) They spend time as they spend money, as though there were no tomorrow.

—It's the wrong question, said Sasha.

Gazing out the third-floor window waiting for the cruise ship to reach its berth against the dank, sour pier, you almost felt like throwing yourself overboard with the galley scraps and tempting the angels to save you. That might have been a loveliness if only you had been spared the rough passage. The tall waves and the swelling sea. A long and bitter night. Alive with thunder and strafing lightning and the howling of the drowning. All imagined in camera. In a thimble on an old teak dresser once upon a time a long time ago before you had even dreamed of time.

—But they are. Even beyond the last hope of imagining. For example: ecstatic redemption. Love given, love received, in mutual rhythms of thrill and calm. Freedom without despair. Youthfulness without stupidity or disintegration. A quiet doom. Those fledglings out of the pocket of whatever had been lost without any hope of being found. Though it seems to be too much to ask for. In its own demented and almost criminal heat.

—Well. One always lives several lives in parallel, you slip between them, from one to the other, fragments that never quite bind into a completely satisfying whole. So we lie to ourselves via the cerebral cortex, medulla, amygdala, brain stem, the requirements of grammar, and our various talents, such as they are, for story-telling, until the whole thing seems to hang together, More or less.

—Like Lincoln's assassins.

—The truth (ignoring the cocky provocation) being too much of an appalling and humiliating mess to be borne, it's quite beneath our dignity. Lincoln indeed.

—So I take what I can use and . . . ?

— . . . and lock the rest in a back cupboard. Never throw any of it away, of course, you never know when it will come in handy. But for heaven's sake, don't take it seriously, it will make you suicidally depressed, and what is depression but a pointless sorrow, one that does not even let you weep. And tears are sorrow's gift, its peculiar pleasure. No. Keep truth under a strong hand and never let it forget who is the boss. You . . .

—Me?

—No. Let me repeat. Keep truth, etc., never let it, etc., who is the boss. Full stop. This side transcendence.

—And what is that, Herr Professor, she asked innocently. Not truth?

He looked at her evasively.

—Again, no. An old and terrifying and yet re-assuring dream of what might be if only we could shape the world's anarchy into something like the heart's desire.

Though that was not what you had said.

—Though even that might be too much to ask for. Such brazen hopes! Life only gives so much sat-isfaction, the rest has to be bargained for under one or two solstice moons. We wander lonely as a cloud but always end up in the same room. Have you ever noticed that? Under the brown lamp and the tussled remnants of an old dress of my aunt's, left to Good Will when the fashions changed. And the woven spell of an itinerant couturier wasn't to be matched by any critic.

—It was really wonderful to see.

—The sparkling waves kept the picture airy and bright as my uncle's nose, don't you know! His brash jokes brought out the best in the family. We fell to with a will at his yearly picnics in Buena Vista park those long afternoons, completely reconciled to the situation, it's so much easier to forget an old wound than in many cases to cure it.

—And it's a lot more fun to laugh!

—When Buddy forgot to snarl and Betty forgot to glare and Judy didn't even bring up that old matter everyone had agreed to forget but no one ever did.

Even Dad was mellow and refrained from sneering at his children. Yes, we were for two and three-quarters of an hour a happy family. Or we thought so, anyway, and isn't that enough, really? As in the old days before the hurricane tore our seaside town to ruins.

—Yes, it was wonderful.

—If by wonderful you mean a total nightmare. Because that's just what she was. The woman never communicated. Well, she "communicated," but only on her own time, when convenient for her schedule. She had no respect for anyone, they could bleed to death if they interfered with one of her episodes or her off-hours between spasms of saintliness. For her a whim was an order from the gods. Sound familiar? Of the female class of the species, if you know what I mean.

—What do you mean?

—The male member hath no self-respect. We always spoil women. Anyway, the lookers. Now feminism has given you the added spice of an eternal grievance. Not only do you get to act badly, you get to feel sanctimonious about it. You get to say, out loud and nasty, you patriarchal male nazi fascist horse's ass scumbag pig, you should be on your knees thanking me for not screwing you to the ground then skinning you alive for the last 10,000 years of masculist oppression, which you are always six inches away from and would love to practice immediately and immoderately upon me right now! Wouldn't you?

—Oh my boy (the other threw in from down the bar), we're such wimps before the feminist, especially when she's hot, we let them run all over us no matter how appallingly they behave. They deserve a hard, long spanking, if you ask me, and you haven't. And not just a little soft S&M before bedtime, no, my darlings, a real beating, to let them know one will not be treated with disrespect at any time, for any reason. It's like anything else, if you let people behave badly, they'll just keep on keeping on. It's true for kids, young men, old men, banks, gangs, corporations, nation states, and females. ("And males!" whispers Sasha, indignantly.) Until they reach the age of 40 and start to lose their looks, or fear they are, when men no longer stare at them whenever they walk into a room, and they start to panic inside, why aren't they looking at me, don't they want me anymore? And she feels for the first time the loss of power as the eyes of men, that bitterly impugned, compulsively desired "male gaze," glide over her like water over a stone and fasten on the face and body of the younger, hotter woman coming up just behind her. At that moment she has a choice. Will she become a spazzy, raging, resentful hysteric or a simple, sweet humble old lady, grateful for the occasional polite smile of a bored but courteous male? Yes, be especially nice to the plain, the old, the ugly ones, they'll be grateful to you, they'll be kind, they will, above all, be loyal. Ignore the hotties if you can. And let them burn. Take the advice of an old male who has been through the wars, whose soul has more scars on it than a naked beekeeper's butt. Of course, no one takes the advice of the old and wise. So you will have to learn the lesson on your own. They call them hot for a reason.

Yes, it sounds familiar. The petulant insecure male brutalizing his local female with reflexive unfairness. Because he had in fact been grossly unfair to her.

—The folly of love, though why one calls love what is a mixture of lust, emotional neediness, misunderstanding and obsession is beyond me.

—To lend it some dignity, I suppose. To hide the raving immodesty of passion. To look less ugly to ourselves in the mirror and the photographs.

—Though that might take more high coloring than a euphemism.

—That abrasion of the mind. That scratch of air and ink on the gray fat of the brain.

—Anything not to have to face it. One does feel foolish when one actually looks at oneself with the pitilessness one usually reserves for others. My God, what am I saying!

—Too much as usual. You'd have been better off keeping your mouth shut. And your pen securely in your pocket.

She giggled haplessly at his ridiculous attempts to ride his cockhorse. He looked down dismayed at Johnson rising lazily to attention in his lap.

Onward, onward!

(—Down, boy, down!)

—But it's so sweet! She almost collapsed in laughter.

("Never call it cute and never call it little!" she remembered her mother telling her. "Not if you want to keep him." "You mean, I can't always tell him the truth?" "Listen to your old mother. Love is based on truth and lies. The trick is getting the right mix. It's like cooking. Salt is truth and lies is pepper. Too much truth you gag, too much lies you'll choke. Honesty in all places at all times, which I know you young people like to go on and on about, is only for people who love themselves more than anybody else." "Oh.")

—That abrasion of the mind.

—"We're stuck on neutral," they had decided one day. "We can't advance and we can't retreat. We can't attack and we can't surrender. We can't lose but we can't win." Though she objected to the military metaphors.

—Object away, be my guest, he'd said amiably. Full speed ahead and damn the torpedoes.

—That's what I mean.

—Yes, yes, I know, I know, but I could barely express myself without military metaphors. And why should your annoyance trump my pleasure, your mild irritation my expressive requirements? Why should I allow your suffering, indeed anyone's suffering, to spoil my feelings of contentment, satisfaction, bliss? If I were sure of an afterlife and a heavenly reward for self-sacrifice and forbearance, I'd say sure, better a delayed gratification than no gratification at all, I would consider denying myself a pleasure an investment in the future, in a permanent state of bliss to come, from simple cost-benefit analysis, but barring that, and I am only certain of how I feel right now and make calculations about my contentment while I am physically alive, and am uncertain, in fact deeply doubtful whether or not, after I am physically excised from planet Earth, I will be "alive" in any meaningful sense (the maggots at the all-you-can eat buffet of my tissues will not count), and feel anything at all between bliss, grief, fury and boredom, I see no reason to forego any happiness, any pleasure, any satisfaction. Here. Now. Any. Whatsoever.

—Unless I threaten to leave you, she said coolly.

—Yes, that would be another matter.

—So, your joy is your right, and my joy is my right, she said in calm and measured tones.

—Exactly.

—And what happens when they conflict?

—Then, he said complacently, we go to war.

—And if you lose?

• • •

The long journey across the widening gulf led in the end to a great vaulted chamber of granite tiling and marble volutes with a crazy blue oeillade that let in gusts of mild summer rain, and they could hear drums and hornpipes and the singing of wedding guests in the narthex and pigeons trapped and muttering in the choir.

—At least once in her life . . .

—Oh yes, it seemed so romantic. And how harsh could it be? Unbearable, apparently . . .

—Love, I insist, had nothing to do with it. Love was tired; a nice hope, a bewitching illusion, but it ended where it began, in the great circle of the bed: fling, birth, fling, death, birth, fling, death, birth, fling. Etc. See? "I love you, I don't love you." They mean practically the same thing . . .

—There wasn't even enough lust to keep the home fires burning. A wave swelled and wiped out half the beach. Just one. It glistened, majestic, the foam along the crown crinkled and sparkled in the sun. A flash and it was over. That was love. A brazen lie, it's quite breathtaking. . . .

—I wish it wasn't so, but there you have it. Like the bird in the bush. The thorn bush. Or was that two birds? The one I had in my hand flew away. After leaving his calling card. That's life. Brazen bird!

—What did you just say?

—I said love had nothing to do with it, as the song put it. Neither then nor now. You had to learn to shake off the weak ruthlessly, they clung to the strong like limpetzs (one of her favorite similes) or bats, sucking their strength as though it were blood, no one was more pitiless than the weak. Shaking them off was the only certain way to make them strong, make them lurch to their feet and bear their burden, and know something like, even if it can never be, deep and abiding contentment. And do it without poisoning the lives of the rest of us. Because this life is the only chance for it I have. Prospects for an afterlife are dim at best, I know I am alive now, and the pleasure or pain of this moment is my only certain knowledge.

—But you just said the heart of happiness is love. So, what of that? she asked, after listening patiently. What if the joy of loving is so deeply gratifying that any pain you feel is infinitely repaid with an ever-deepening satisfaction, a profound and never-ending hope?

He looked into her eyes with an almost frightening sorrow.

You see through me. You're blessed if that is true. And I'm—well, not. I feel like a butterfly with charred wings. I sit on the ground watching the other butterflies fluttering, flower to flower, above my head, and I build my cold philosophy to shield myself from resentment and hatred and bitterness. Love if you are able to, and know the deepest joys life can offer, even in the teeth of its pain. If, like me, you can't love, clutch your little pleasures, satisfactions of the moment, hours of serenity, days of tranquility, and let everyone else go hang. Your pleasures will be weak, your happiness thin, but your suffering will be thin too, your pain weak, your strongest feelings numb. Let everyone seek the joys he can bear and hold onto them with all his might.

—Or "her," she reminded him sharply.

—You can't get off your high horse for a second, he said, with a wry look, can you, my darling?

Her eyes held him for a moment like the shackles of his own explanation.

—Make them lurch to their feet, indeed!

A curtal sonnet. A linnet's wing. A singing au pair. A surge into the abyss.

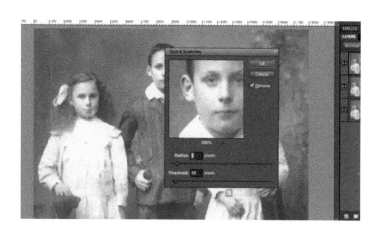

The scop struck his thigh, and the siege towers rolled toward the closed gates. His peers stood in long rows along the wall tops, their bows arched toward heaven. The morning was bright, there was a light wind from the forest, the clatter of carts could be heard in the distance. A falcon hovered above the tower. Streaks of cloud faded like smoke between the hills. Time froze, as time will. The messenger had already departed. He had pressed his seal on the wax. The sea itself bore the mark of its own passing, it rode the foam like a conqueror. It was the present that had always been an illusion. The future was a dark eye staring without seeing you as it advanced backward into the darkness ahead. Only memory was real, it caught the moment in its web like a spider. History was the empire where man was a king, every woman a goddess full of a sweet, sly joy. If only it could have been kept up for more than a season of childhoods. The maw of time ate at its own tail. The reptiles froze too in the winter slime, their eyes shocked with melting fire. The arrows shot in a black, arching rain, and a crowd of howls rose from the land as they fell.

The falcon remained still above the tower. At the bottom of the gully lay a small dark form curled up like pity. Between the two was a wall of stale air. Clouds hung like torn sheets from the battlements. The sun gave it a sharp glance, then moved to other battlefields. It was appalling what fools our spies were. They took on trust the slightest appeals to their humiliated paranoia and harvested black flocks of the innocent. It was heresy to say so, of course, more in some cases than one's life was worth. At the very least you might lose several years of seniority in the camera oscura of a rattling and deconstructed bureaucracy. Candor always being a blistering virtue.

—That heals in direct proportion to its sting.

The catamaran swelled over the bow a sail as white as her thighs, followed by a wing hard as a fuselage and noisy as an ungreased pulley hoisting an elephant. You anoint it the palace of our future, where the gold will penetrate the night like a monkey's poisoned eye.

—I would seriously consider rephrasing that line. For the e-book version, at least.

—I love thee more than life itself, but, sweetheart, I do hate it when you piss on my verbiage.

And there will be no e-book version. Or only over my dead body.

—Sorry, but somebody has to bring you back to earth.

—For God's sake, why?

—But don't you want to have any readers?

—I'm not sure I do. I have you, don't I? And you are the most passionate reader I know. When you love it, you adore it , and when you hate it, you hate it to the point of shrieking lunacy. Only the NSA reads with your passion. You read it—you pay attention, which is more than anyone else has ever done—and that is all that counts. It's as good as the old KGB, from what my Russian friends tell me! Their greatest despair about democracy was that they could publish anything they wanted, and nobody gave a damn. Thank God for Vlad! Not a moment too soon. A writer needs only one reader—the reader who reads him as a matter of life or death.

Burn this book after reading. It is the only way you will never forget it.

—Not that he didn't enjoy it, he did, very much indeed, went on, after an interval, the portly man, it was that he couldn't bear making it a part of his relationships. So his relationships were simple and direct. He was lucky in that, in his childhood, he'd never been made to feel that spanking the monkey was so terrible. A serious lapse on the side of his parents.

Once his mother tried to convince him (by exceedingly oblique references) otherwise, but it was by then far too late; he'd had many years of practice to prove to his own satisfaction that there were no untoward consequences (stunted growth? madness? retardation? Then why am I tall for my age and near the top of my class? Well, at least not at the bottom . . .)

In later years, he occasionally missed the feeling of a woman's body under his hands.

If I get desperate, I'll hire a hooker, he thought.

The relationship between hooker and client is clear, clean, neat: money for sex for money. No commitment issues, manipulation, dishonesty. All sex should be so clear, so easy, so nice! Remove sex from relationships! Remove sex from marriage! Sex without relationship! A heaven-sent idea! From a God who really understands human beings!

He never grew desperate: the internet saved him from that. Going solo with a porn video was altogether more dependable than the "real thing": cheaper and, with HD, quite as vivid. You could have as many women as you could manage, day in, day out. And the girls were far prettier than anyone he would have to pay for.

When he told Sasha all of this, she wasn't even shocked. The pieces fell into place and displayed the profile of his life with an enigmatic clarity.

—I always wondered why you took so long to

touch me, she said. At first I thought you were gay. But you didn't seem interested in men. You didn't seem interested in anyone. I thought it might be revenge.

—Maybe it was, he said. Though I can't remember the crime. By the way, it's not true I wasn't interested in anyone. I have always been profoundly interested in myself. That is supposed to be the height of immorality. But frankly I don't see it. It's like masturbating: by the time people were warning me against it, I had been practicing it for so long, I knew it had no bad consequences at all.

He had a point. The greatest evil comes from two sorts of people: those who require a partner in sex (and often, naturally, don't have one, or when they have one, either lose it, or are in danger of losing it, and therefore have a constantly renewed grievance against life in general for placing them in this cruel position), and those who profess to be selfless (but of course that is precisely what a person cannot be, without a self they would be dead; their self-division makes them hypocrites and hate every human being who, with ingenuous frankness, adores himself).

—So, it was not self-centeredness but self-less-ness, and it was not self-abuse but "love," that created much of the evil human beings inflict on each other?

—It's a toss-up who are the most evil people

in the world: the humble, modest and meek, or the rich, the powerful, the arrogant.

—Perhaps they create each other.

No, he never grew desperate. Or at least not enough.

—I would still seriously consider rephrasing it. Such as: Caught there, down in the weeds. In the wet autumn weather. When the skies are gray and silent except for the sound of the rain. A smattering of birdcalls just before the birds leave for the south. The dull and sleepy fog in the little valley where the pines are still so fragrant.

You could almost smell the deep mud and grassy smell of time passing, or rather standing still, like a pool in the middle of the woods. With here and there a late flower, white or blue, in the damp shadows. And behind the tapping of the water against the leaves, silence. Such comfort even in the cold. As though you were sheltered. Safe. Loved. "Nature," you would whisper. "This is nature." You thought you had found your god, your religion was the perfectly obvious, it was simply worship of reality, reality was nature, it was humankind that created "unreality" (as if "unreality' could exist! Not unreality, then: the lie.) Reality was your temple. Your deepest secret. How old were you, nine, ten? Was this the revelation?

—Or the innocence?

—What is innocence? What is revelation? I'm not being rhetorical here. I have wrestled with these questions all my life, and usually ended up screaming on the mat. The adult, though better informed than the child, and sometimes even cleverer, forgot the little wisdom he once had: that he is a small, vulnerable, mortal piece of the cosmos, like a crystal of sugar, or a drop of liquid, though a piece gifted, or cursed, with awareness; caught, that is, in the illusion of separateness (that is what awareness, consciousness, is: an illusion of separateness that is just close enough to reality to give it manipulative power: a useful illusion; consciousness is the first lie).

In your slyness and cunning you forget the great, pale truths that were once clear to you. You exchange illusions, trade blindnesses, lose one stupidity while gaining another. Above all, you forget the wisdom of the weak in your intoxication with your little conquests of power. Don't you think?

—Yes, said Sasha, for once I do, and smiled with only a touch of irony. Think, that is. Even agree.

Such comfort even in the cold. You remember how it was. The matches kept for the porch light, and the slightly oily residue in the ashtray. For the locks, without graphite, became stiff. A modicum of sanity was all that was needed. And they didn't always get it even then. A toast to a tree and other augurs of happiness! The swallows canted over the roof with startling cartwheels. The blue jay nattered and flexed its wings like a pair of banners. The owl pooh-poohed the lateness of the hour. And the immense strongbox was clamped shut with a proper wheeze. So there! So what! So now!

—I repeat: a modicum of sanity was all that was needed. More than that and we'd've drowned in gravy. Too sane is too sane, you might as well be crazy. And too much intelligence just makes you cocky and depressed. Look at the world, now. Drop your silly book. Yes, yes, the one now in your hands. You can't tell me it isn't a wonder: the table under your hand, the quilt, the blanket, the lap of your trousers, your bathing suit, your skirt. There's a window over there, stand up and walk over to it. Look. (I know: I'm a bully. Just do it, and we'll be out of here all the sooner.)

What do you see?

(Yes, yes, write it down—I'm sorry, please write it down, in the small space below: a list of things you see (hear, smell, taste, touch) when you look out the window. Take your time. We are in no great hurry. The list can be as long or short as you like. After all, this is now your book. Or, if you're feeling too lazy, just look around you. That's right. There's a world out there. Listen to the lazy Christmas blues coming through the café sound system: it's Ella, I'm sure it is.)

From where I sit I see the following:

The interior of a west coast café, with seismic support beams making a graceful right-angled triangle in the middle of the room.

Numerous café chairs, a dozen tables of various shapes and sizes, most of them occupied by leisurely eating and chatting lunchers (most are in couples, with a few small groups, and several loners seriously addressing their plates; there is a common table with several loners exaggeratedly ignoring each other behind their open lap tops); two iron railings lead up to the café's glass door through a wall of glass looking out onto the street.

Passing cars, a truck, bus, males and females bustling, pacing, stalking by at businesslike gaits (mostly adults, a few adolescents, no children), two small, abandoned-looking trees across the street, the entrance to a parking garage with a sign flashing in red ("CAR COMING"), a cat sleeping on a backpack near the curb (no sign of the owner), three, no four, pigeons pecking in the gutter a few feet from the sleeping cat, the entrance to a 7-11, the aggressively hip windows of a Banana Republic, two narrow green doors in a wall, shut except for one that seems invitingly ajar, several open laptops, three smartphones being swiped or tapped by anxious-looking teenagers, three ballpoint pens held by two students and a tourist (the pen in my hand is the fourth), a V-neck sweater and two turtlenecks, two white quilt parkas, a business suit holding a briefcase in swift passage across the view, shadowy reflections across the street, sun, clouds, sky (just barely visible if I stretch forward and look up).

I smell: coffee, cloves, cinnamon, pastry custard, bread.

I feel: the press of corduroy against my legs. The squeeze of a vest against my torso. The rub against my wrist of my new watchband.

I taste: . . .

—And that's just a handful of almost wholly in-adequate words (Shakespeare I am not) scribbled on a piece of paper. Uniqueness slips through words like mercury; they reduce everything to a class. They are like the internet. The internet reduces the universe and everything in it to an image on a screen; in other words, to the internet. Language reduces the universe and everything in it to a string of words; in other words, to itself. And we end up believing our words even though our own senses scream at us that our words are hopelessly wrong. Language is always in danger of turning us into nihilists. There once was a young philosopher who worked out a logically impeccable argument that proved, without possibility of error, that there was no such thing as the sun. He went over his arguments again and again, but the logic was ironclad, and there was no escaping the conclusion that the sun, not only did not exist, but could not possibly exist. He broke down and wept.

It would have been no use to go outside and look up. And believe his eyes. No: the logic was impeccable. The sun did not exist.

—And burn his papers, she added.

—What?

—Go outside, look up, go inside, burn his papers. And end the insanity of reason, she said.

—But I love words, he objected. They're my little darlings.

—Kill your darlings, she said, as the fool in creative writing class ordered you.

—No, he replied. Let them live. But always remind them who is boss.

—End the insanity of reason, no doubt! said the portly man. That had always been a pet project of his. Not that it required success across the culture, he having given up on his own "culture" a long time ago. It was a question principally of saving his soul. And help save those of a few of friends, though he had no desire to impose on them. They might see, or they might not. It wasn't his business to grind their lenses for them and poke their eyes full of insights. After all, he wasn't so sure he was right; he was probably as wrong as everybody else, more likely even more wrong as he probably had too much confidence in his brain.

His own personal salvation, however, that he felt

(despite the evidence, to say nothing of two thousand years of philosophy) might just be within his grasp: he might be able, in effect, to force God's hand. He was a Pelagian enough to consider that: he would shame God into saving him. He would be the insect that, in the act of being smashed by the divine palm, defied it. It would be the sincerest expression of his faith. He would lead an exemplary life (whatever that was). He would say, at the end of it: see what I have done with the life you gave me, I have done some good with it – nothing grand, I admit, little good things in small doses, in little packages of honesty, creation, love, even tenderness—I have grown flower and fruit, built a home and a shrine, drawn a few moments of beauty from the air, the earth, voice and skin , ink and paper, in celebration of life and earth and of their timeless creator; and whatever evil I have done (for who can avoid doing his share of evil in this world? Every life is built on the death and suffering of others), the evil I have done has been little more than the inevitable residue that every life leaves behind it; in fact, much of the evil I have done has done more damage to me than to anyone else. I have kept faith with you, with beauty and goodness and truth, even when I failed, and failure is woven into the being of the world you have created; more from luck than merit, I have fought the worst temptations and managed to avoid the worst evils, I and those like me, and there are many of us, I speak not only for myself, who have earned our salvation, I give you my soul and heart, battered and stained as they are, but also a little richer with a few crumbs of knowledge and the brightness of a many thousand sunrises, and I hope something that might be almost confused with a shade of wisdom, for I have made mistakes and errors in untold numbers, but have learned from them beyond, I hope, the bitterness of their first lessons, and still am able to love your creation even though it has wounded me and many others (my sufferings have been bearable, but the sufferings of others have not always been) at least as often as it has caressed us, and still I am able to love you, creator of the universe, the metaverse, the eternal world, as of myself and us. I ask you to save us. For we are lost and stumble in the darkness raving and hurt and angry, cruel in our misery and even crueler in our happiness. We are lost, injured, bent and crooked under the burden of living. Save us. Please. Save us all. Even those of us who have failed and seem without any possibility of redemption. Who hate you and all your works, despise humanity, and loathe and detest the world itself. Who have given up on you and curse you from the bottom of their hearts. Take us to you, even so. Embrace us. Show us more love than we have ever shown you. Make us cry from joy.

She was silent where she sat in the darkness, overhearing him praying. She could hardly believe her ears. It made her almost believe. Correction: it made her almost want to believe. It was an hour before dawn. Then the sun rose. And, as has been known to happen, the light dispersed the ecstasy as though it had never been.

If he could only discover what it was. The pebble on the windowsill, the slack call of the snowy owl, the waste of time in the long welter of personal loss. An unseemly business no one had ever heard of before. A few black strato-nimbus clouds crossing the crowning cumulus and the cold hard blue behind it.

—I call down the long dark corridor. You hear nothing at the end but the sound of water dripping into a pair of cupped hands. The silence was almost blinding. I keep telling you but nothing seems to sink in. Because you seem to hear only what you already know. Is that it then— the curse of it, trying to communicate with you? Well? Do you think we have a chance?

The storm came up from the southeast. It blew down three hundred trees in a dozen parks across the midwestern city. More than you had thought possible. The town staggered like a drunk through the nightfall, the air smelled of resin for weeks. And the fires could be seen from as far as Warren. They told you on Sunday you could have known sooner if your cellphones hadn't been singing music from the last century. And you had been so certain that technology would save you. In its black, frowzy gown. The connection was so alive—it almost melted in your hand.

—We have a chance, though barely. Had a chance. Now gone, of course, like so many others.

And again I call down the corridor. But nothing springs from the cages. The nihilist followed his luck when it came, pried the stones from the wellhead and sucked on the mortar in the frost. What was it again that you don't believe? In anything. Rather much! Even winter believes in snow. Though he had not seen snow in years. He wondered how he'd react to it now that his hair was entangled in the grass.

A curt and haughty robin twittered and sprang from the ink-black pines. You do not know what happened next but your gentle reader might. It's why you cannot speak of the present—you have no perspective on it. It's all a bright-walled blackness. You keep stumbling on the threshold of a door that will not open. You hardly know where you have been. There may even be a way out. Expectancy is a long disappointment. Something makes no noise while passing through a distant room. Why can't you hear her? Is she still there?

She looked anxiously down the hall but could only hear the pattering of disappearing feet. Like dust.

—Insist on knowing. You will tell me, and I will know. I shall. I must. In all.

Tirelessly he labors at the high cliff face. Working through the granite with his fingernails, for lack of other tools. His fingers bleed when he's overzealous. You would think he'd be making more progress, after all he's been at it for years. Surprising how little. A few inches of bloody rock, a small alcove, just big enough to fit his body in. But how proud of those inches he is! He dreams of a son to carry on the work when he's gone. Though he has no son. He dreams of a spiritual son to carry it on. Knowing nothing of who that might be. And he stares at the shallow ditch in the rock with its traces of blood from his own hands in despair. A door, not a grave, he prays.

—Some atheist, the atheist laughs.

—Nihilum ex nihilo, quips the nihilist.

What after all did you expect? That someone would hand you a key? He doesn't answer but goes back to his scratching scratching scratching till his fingers are bloody again. The rack after all is holy, the blood is proof. Isn't it? The pain theory of value. The nihilist continues to listen with a bright-eyed smile. But he laughs gently.

—So, says Sasha, referring to the current situation in the country, in the world. What are you going to do about it? Anything? Aside from whining.

—What is there to do? I could hardly murder the president!

—Hardly, she says dryly.

You call down the long dark corridor. There is an echo, then not even that. A sound of crumbling, then a sigh, then a long deep boom.

The fall of an ancient city, its tall flames shining on the surface of a lake as black as the night above it, far from the haunts of the owl and the petrel and the hard-bearing joints of the cloven ice. The smoke hiding the great armies of the stars and the mindless, staring moon. Where were you when all that started? You've always known how to make yourself scarce. Fearlessness was never your virtue. Unless it was a marker of split tabs and barroom testimonials. And other dire and implausible schemes. Admit it. There is no modern myth that claims too much for you. You even season the belly's appetite with— read it!—moldy cheeses. The pleroma is waiting for you, sagging like an accidental pregnancy. But who knows? I landed the last fish before the pond froze over. Now it's as flat as a table. Can I share, she asked? I only want to be able to see you and hear your voice when you grumble on the phone and smell your smell, it gives me so much peace. He gazed at her with a deeply hurt look. I detest being reminded of my body. I have spent my life doing everything I can to forget I have one. To forget the accursed fact I am one. And then you have to say that. But that is what I am supposed to say. You were supposed to say I don't think we can even be friends. With that terrible smile of yours, so charming and brutal. And so slowly kill my heart. And then you ask me why I hate you. The gall. I hate you because I loved you. Because it keeps me alive.

If he could discover what that was. The bone of contention having long been gnawed hollow.

—Like a penny pipe whistling during spring break. With a heave-ho!

The storm eats the shoreline of the continent then paces in long gales into the interior, where, blind with snow, it kicks an abandoned city to pieces. The hills across the lake are flooded with refugees, the valleys drown in the rainfall. And nothing can be seen in the dancing night. The foam spits in the camera's eye and the image is forsaken in an instant. No picture, no evidence. If it's not on video, it never happened. The chaos of the sea meets the chaos of the land in a long, poisoned embrace.

From the blackness of space it looked like the icing on an enormous cake, a blanc-mange spread with a butterknife over a vast, succulent blueberry. Catastrophe offered by the mindless ocean to the mindless continent.

—What a spectral thwarting of man's decency and pride!

The cotton-candy stand ripped to shreds at the first blow. The ancient pier wrecked in a shattering white swipe. The old river ferry beached and broken. The pavilion taken up and twirled in an old-fashioned dance, then cast aside into the blasted shipyard for the next intoxicated partner. The boardwalk wrecked and floated, a raft at a time, out the rocking tide.

A dog barks frantically somewhere between the beach and the dark horizon.

The absurd and scornful pity of it.

Then the fist shaking at the sky and raising the invisible tower.

To end the insanity of reason.

—Perfect strokes for perfect blokes. Blowhard windbags in the bar scene, voguing and mou'ing in the clubs, you really should have been there, I'm tellin' you. But forget it, there's no getting through to you . . .

The ice was three inches thick on the river between Trenton and Washington's Crossing. That night, of all nights, the darkest in years, the stars snuffed out like the candles on an only child's birthday cake, the moon black as the cracks in the ice. I shiver just thinking about it. The grease smudge on my hand. The sound of the oars in the oarlocks. The rust between my fingers. The acid at the back of my tongue. Expectations were too high, and the mourning afterward lasted for months. A rustling of dry roses on the kitchen sill. A game of tag in the junkyard. A smell of compost in the fall.

—Listen! I think it's a whip-poor-will.

—"Whip, poor Will!"

Silence.

—"Whip, poor Will!"

Silence.

—"Whip, poor Will!"

Deep under the sand there is an ancient anchor. No one knows where it is buried. By the dunes they found a doll house, the little pieces of furniture were scattered over the sand. A seagull crossed the sun like an open hand.

—A modicum of sanity is sometimes all we need, she said softly. Sometimes not even that.

Though it takes slightly more to catch the tailings from a coal pit and line them up like dead cinders from a long-forgotten fire. And light them again as if memory were a miracle as fine as the raising of Lazarus, and indeed it is—matter remembering is almost as astonishing as matter coming up with "So What?" or "Guernica" or fractal theory. Or the iPad. Yet, if they last in the mind alone, do they last indeed? Because, if it happens once, it happens forever. Some might find that reassuring, others an unendurable nightmare.

The clanging buoy on the wind-beaten bay. The waves slipping between the pilings near the gully. The scent of decomposing oysters.

—Sigh, he said. Just once for me. I can hear you from the chair in the corner. Why are you weeping? You're in America, after all.

—But that is why I am weeping. It's true even here.

—What is true?

—Everything.

The rain slips down the windowpanes. They meet and they break apart and they meet again. They live in a kind of hushed expectancy. The glass is cold to the touch but not unpleasant. The gray sky hides the scars. And the dawn is always ready like a secret amulet in your pocket.

—Be brave, my darling. Look. I'm holding the sun in my palm.

Such comfort even in the cold.

—The dream I can just remember forgetting. The woman appearing in it, like that famous French actress I always liked, Juliette Binoche, not quite as

118

seriously beautiful perhaps, but lovely enough, oh yes, who, part of a couple apparently, parted from the couple on meeting me, whispering behind me, "I've fallen in love with him," and me feeling tickled but taking it just a bit for granted, then a moment later, I show up at her apartment, talking about everything and nothing, but seeing how happy this lovely woman is to see me, at one point gesturing her to come to me, but she protesting she isn't on the pill. Nothing like that has ever happened to me in real life, heaven knows, most women avoid me like the plague; they won't even talk to me let alone try to seduce me, which is why I once thought I hated them (the truth is I loved them too much for my own good, I got far too excited in their company, then I realized it and went mum, and there I am, either blathering like a spaz or frozen stock still, hypnotized by their beauty, either way it puts them off—but I have to take some revenge for their hostility, their indifference, their sexual disgust: that is the real war between the sexes: the childish "I loathe you more than you loathe me"). Where had that dream come from? I have a guess but I'm almost afraid to acknowledge it, even to myself.

—Underneath your pride, the arrogance glittering from your appraising eyes, the body language of self-affirmation, the gestures proclaiming your superiority, you are in fact forever laughing at your own pretentions, you think it a great joke that other people take you far more seriously than you take yourself, in your own eyes you are just an ordinary fellow, vain and fallible and selfish, though with a strain of common sense and decency that prevents you from ever causing deliberate injury to another living thing. That's the real source of your pride. Not that you love people, you don't—you find most human beings stupid, deluded, deceitful, predatory, self-absorbed ("Yes, I'm awful—but you still love me, don't you?"). But you can't bear the thought of hurting them.

This is too much explanation, it explains nothing. The one image of the dream that lasted in his memory was of her soft middle-aged face looking just past him and slightly above as though catching a glance at herself in a mirror across the room or lost in a sweet fading thought. Not looking at him. He looking at her. Contented. Quiet. Happy. He in her. She in him.

—I would seriously consider rephrasing that line.

—About what?

—About what happened after he left and the lights went out and despair fell over them like a winter night. How cruel the withdrawal of goodness can be. It can feel greater even than the advent of evil. The closing of the door of love. There is no cold quite like that cold. Even death seems not so savage. So you might want to reconsider it, I think.

He held the letter up in his bandaged hand and gazed at it absent-mindedly.

—Perhaps I will, he said at last. After all, there's more than one way out. Though none that doesn't inflict pain on someone. For a long time afterward you'll feel the phantom heart beating in the place where it once sat in your ribcage behind the sternum between the two still miraculously breathing lungs. It will take some time but eventually it will fill with warm shadows. And you will no longer be cursed with happy memories. But we anticipate, he said.

—No, she said, you do.

A falcon hovered above the town.

—But really there was nothing between them, nothing but air, though he'd always hoped there might be. Something more substantial, that is.

—Like a glass of lemonade on a summer porch or a breeze off the ocean at nightfall?

—Well, something you could almost hold but that didn't hold you. That passed off with a smile and a strange pale look, like a dropped petal on a coffee table or the memory of a yellow rose in the darkening evening. The one he almost gave her but was afraid of the message it told, it seemed so stark. Love, after all, was a terrible thing. Its small hand was heavy as the world.

But he never grew desperate enough.

And so the moment passed into history. The empire declined into decadence, the barbarians overwhelmed the borders, the cities burned beside the oceans, the flames reflected in the night sky for miles out to sea. The emperor wept in his lunacy, he had taken himself for a god. And the master of the universe stood staring in the streets, babbling between long silences of his days of money and power, but above all money. And now the money could buy nothing: its ashes fluttered up like black butterflies from the conflagration.

—I was richer than God, I was king of the world before DiCaprio was out of diapers. I bought two presidents of the United States, half the Congress and three Supreme Court justices.

The bruised mouth is flecked with saliva, the crazy eye is yellow as pus, the body stinks of urine and sweat.

—You think I'm crazy. You think I'm lying. But these hands brought Wall Street to its knees.

The king passes by, with his knights in tow. He is riding a red wagon being pulled by a fat man, his followers hobble by on crutches singing "Material Girl" at the top of their lungs.

—Make them stand on their own two feet, he said hoarsely. That will give them some sense. It's time to get over ehpatay-ing the bourgeoisie, the avant-garde is long past its prime. The winter of a long senescence is the gift of a childhood never out-lived. Peter Pan was no fool. There are no adults in the room. Even if there were, it wouldn't save you. More wisdom is lost between the ages of nine and thirteen than is made up for in the next six decades. I've read mountains of books by the world's greatest minds, and not one has a convincing answer. The best they do is shrug before the darkness toward which we gather. I was almost sixty before I was as smart as I was at ten.

—Your strange conclusion, my love?

—It's strange that one can ever have known. Puberty has a lot to answer for. It's an embarka-tion for idiocy. The beauty of the hour sounds like a gong, but softly. Behind every dead rose is the spring's promise of a magnificent garden. We lived in a cave of wonder. Every eye was an emperor's court, every mind a palace, the universe our crown. My little ignorant mortal self was like a drop of the sea in which suns moved on mysterious and urgent journeys. I could be sure of nothing but that I inhab-ited a ragged miracle more vast than space and time, beyond even the godlike human brain. I have been drunk on hope. I have been drunk on despair. I have been high on vanity and pride. I have been crazy with bitterness. My universe creates unendingly, then takes it all back. And then, the sly joker, creates even more. Forever. Multiverses! And that's just the beginning!

It's like a capitalist factory running on ecstasy, steroids, acid and crystal meth—an immense laboratory of unending novelty. Eternity is just the way it is. Look at the end of your index finger—yes, look at it. There. See? Infinity spiraling in 5,000 dimensions. More or less. And you don't think that you and God are brothers! You are an atheist? That only means you have lost faith in yourself. My conclusion? What could that possibly matter! There is no conclusion.

—You're a child, she said affectionately. That is your conclusion.

—Scion of a castle of matter, energy and chance. If only my stupid brain could state it. Sometimes I feel we human beings are like children locked in a room at the far end of a huge house, just able to hear what the adults are doing at the other end, and we spend our time guessing what they are up to but never knowing for sure. We dress up like adults and pose and preen and make war and speeches and kill each other in the name of the voices, garbled and indistinct, that we think we hear, and we behave like crazies and fools because we never know for certain and can't face the simple fact that we cannot even be sure we are locked in our childhood room and must make do. The room has a window, and the view—sometimes ravishingly beautiful, sometimes viciously ugly, sometimes a crashing bore—is constantly changing. We are like spectres locked inside inadequate bodies.

—And the universe is ours. Have you ever noticed, you self-absorbed little man? We "own" nothing, despite those lies called laws, but everything we see, hear, taste, touch, smell is our possession. I see the sun, I possess the sun. I look at the sky, I own the sky. If you buy a Lamborghini, you possess it when you see it, touch it, handle it, smell it; the moment you walk away from it, you abandon it, it abandons you. It may as well not even exist.

No one can live a life of sensation alone—seeing hearing smelling touching tasting.. Of paying attention. The holiest of holies. The vita contemplativa. Even if we should. Even for a monk, life is a barrage of distractions: make supper, clean up, cut the grass, sweep the stairs, milk the cows, take a bath, ring in matins—then every so often you're allowed to pray.

—But we can, she said. We can discipline ourselves, of course. Even if it happens only once a day, it will reveal the splendor of our lives, the miracle of our godlike existence, our kinship with transcendence. The great secret, which is that we are gods, however small and far down in the hierarchy of the heavens.

—Gods? I looked at you, Sasha, with (he could feel it on his face) a smile. Ghosts, more like it.

—You shouldn't look so surprised. We can't be ghosts without being gods. You'd agree human beings can be demons.

—Have I seen the news today?

—And a demon is a vicious, little god. So you actually do believe me, though you don't realize it yet.

—Well, he smiled, I'll be damned.

—More to the point . . . though, if I want to sound official, I should put on my wings, hover over your head and sing, in great choirs: "Nay, Mortal— Thou Shalt Be Saved!"

—Nice to know angels have a sense of the ridiculous after all.

—What do you think we do in heaven all day—sing hymns and read sermons to each other? You're confusing us with hell. We spend much of our time dreaming up jokes – especially about the Old Man. It tickles him pink. You should hear him laugh. Have you heard the one about God coming into a bar? He's sitting there, griping to the bartender: "Technology!" he says. "I keep saying 'Fiat lux, fiat lux!' and the damned light still doesn't go on!" I thought he'd die laughing at that one.

Love had nothing to do with it, as the song said. It was all about something in her eyes. They never let you in, and yet they didn't shut you out completely either. Like the prayers that were her hands. No one knew who knew Sasha, because no one really did. Yet everyone was drawn to her. She became for many of us a craving, like a drug. Her beauty was the heroic kind that turned strong men into bumbling adolescents, whimpering children, and just confused everyone else. She resented her own beauty (he could feel it). It kept lying to other people: it said I love you when she felt no love for them and I hate you when she felt no hatred. It crowded her, turned the silence she craved into a long shouting match, the darkness she loved into a display of fireworks that wore her out with their continual, compulsive brilliance.

—I know you love me but leave me alone for a while, a year, a lifetime.

She learned the hard way that beauty comes with a penalty: stares like a constant punishment.

—Everyone loves me, she said once in despair.

—No, he said, everyone wants you. I love you. And so I shall go away. Even though losing your company breaks my heart and reduces me to moaning in the night. You will probably not believe this, but I'm going to say it anyway. You were the one who introduced me to happiness. You taught me the meaning of joy. I thought I had known before. But I hadn't, not the ghost of it. Happiness comes with loving you and knowing I am loved by you. Joy is being in the same room with you, in your arms, in the air that surrounds you. But I can give up joy. I don't really need to see you. Seeing you is a joy that almost intimidates me. I never need to see you, if that is what you want. Loving you is all the happiness I need. I can go on living if I have that—that is what I mean. I will have a reason to live. I can give up that joy if I can keep that happiness.

But she had already gratefully closed the door. And, for safe measure, locked it.

—And I thought you said love had nothing to do with it! Liar, she smiled, hidden in the silence and the dark.

—That's exactly what I mean. When I mean anything at all.

He was speaking between drags on a prominent cigarette. (He was still smoking then.)

—Ineffable, oracular, mildly ridiculous. Like an old world European installed in his corner at the café, burbling charming lunacies to gullible students, mostly female, whose minds had been tamed by a childhood spent between ministers, matriarchs and classroom martinets. Until their brains were well and completely cooked. In a manner of speaking.

He exhaled elaborately and let the smoke sign the air with his meaning.

—Underneath his sweetness he was an arrogant so-and-so, I always knew it. Self-centered to a fault.

—What else could you expect from someone who signed his letters with his blood?

The sunset raised an immense pink curtain above the view over the park, between the closing day's eye and the evening star, Venus shivering in the twilight.

—You can almost count them as they appear. One . . . two . . . It's curious. Anything rather than nothing. The Higgs boson answers nothing. Why the Higgs boson? And why the thing that caused the Higgs boson? And why the thing that caused that? And on and on and on, infinitely. Aristotle's logical reduction. There's no more explanation in that than in the Old Testament or the bleariest shaman's rants. It comes down to faith, whether in the guts of an owl or equations on a white board and simulations on a YouTube video. There is no "universally persuasive reason," O Socrates, and no "self-evident truth," René; just prejudice and rhetoric, acquiescence and browbeating, and the liberation, and hell, of eternal questioning without answers. No foundations, just sand all the way down, as some British philo unhelpfully put it.

—I wouldn't be so sure. We may just not have found the right method yet. We have gotten to the moon, Mars, Saturn. We're sailing beyond Neptune, past poor demoted Pluto. One day we may even get to a universally persuasive reason and a self-evident fact: a foundation after all. There. You can see Orion lift his leg over the horizon, his sword raised bravely among the stars.

That abrasion of the mind. The spontaneity that prose is supposed to exhibit. Even a poem however rigidly constructed. I mean, rigorously. Unavailable, now, of course, that he's beyond anything like that. The cart before the horse was always his weakness.

Elect even among the stars scintillating against a dusty blue background. The flats stuck at the sides half way into the wings. The cables hanging like swags and lianas tangled and tarry above the stage planks. The crew racing around to replace them with flimsy props, garish decorations, tawdry machinery and painted actors to make up for the disappointments of reality. Which is after all shabby, empty, humiliating and fatal. The intensity of that gaze across two centuries. Holding you rapt in its dream. It's a kind of perfection precisely because it does not pretend to mirror reality, no, it's all artifice, that is its reality, its truth—its integrity, if you will, or even if you won't. It sails on without us, we wave to it as it moves toward the horizon, a diminishing spread of dark sails against the gathering offshore fog. Into which it vanishes with a turn and a glance back at us, like a young, first-time ballerina, a tremulous and unbelieving smile on her stage-frightened, hopeful, childlike face.

Sound typical? Whatever it was he never understood about women (for example), or the saner ones he had known. Though picking them out from the crazy was not always easy. None were innocent, though some were, in the deepest sense, good, loving and true—far nicer than us, heaven knows! Women are generous when they love, whereas men, when we love, take.

—But never the sexy ones.

—Well, yes, to be sure. What was it about those?

—Many are too beautiful in their own eyes (she said, putting on her lecture cap), they despise anyone who falls for them. As though falling for them were a sign of weakness, and there is nothing we despise more. Because we know our beauty is a deception and a trap. Beauty is a pledge of joy, of love, but all a woman's beauty promises is a kind of tiger trap above which a smile hovers, like bait.

—Vagina dendata! Con de Narcisse!

—We are, all of us, predators, we can't help yourselves. Predators of virtue. Programmed to find a mate to provide for us and our offspring. Though I don't intend either to marry or have children, she said coolly.

He laughed in the dim café. (What is café philosophy without a café?)

—You think our genes care what "we" have decided? Our glands are programmed in DNA code, switches going off and on due to circumstances, chance, things over which we have no control—do you have the gene for Alzheimer's, for Parkinson's, MS? do you want to know you are almost certain to become a bug-eyed gaga drooling clot of human tissue living in an eternal present and bankrupting family, society, country? But do we have any say in the matter? Biochemistry is fate. It frames everything we are. Just as everything men do is framed to penetrate the female's defenses and drop your seed inside us. We can't help ourselves, you can't help yourselves. If you can't break through the female's defenses, you start breaking everything else. And so you guys enjoy blowing things up. We pilot our drives between massacres of hormones, between the slaughter of mortality and the nets of generation, until the ocean swallows us.

—That's what our epoch taught us (he said, after a pause). It was considered hard, inescapable fact, the bedrock reality of us and the world—harsh and brutal, even cruel, but real. The Truth. Anyone who disagreed was a liar, a criminal, possibly a Nazi. We are ruled by a god, and that god is the selfish gene. Beauty, love, the ideal, faith and goodness and truth—all of them are no more than masks to lure us into the pit of reproduction. Reproduce, no matter what, is the iron law. The theory was elegant, simple, profound; it answered every question, solved every problem. The only difficulty was that it left clenched, like a gauntlet on a coffee table, an absolute despair.

He stared at the rain beginning on the sidewalk outside the window.

—Then (he continued) we realized maybe that "the hard truth" had no more "truth" in it than the libraries it had so ingloriously stripped, humiliated and jettisoned; that it was, from the ground up, in fact a smug, self-serving and ignominious mistake, just one more of humanity's elaborate, ponderous and inconceivably ridiculous ideas about the cosmos, no more worth taking seriously than Aristotle's mechanics or medieval cosmology or the latest

135

papal bull. A theoretical house of cards, a barrage of weak logic, falsified evidence, intellectual intimidation, threats against dissidence, political oppression and petty revenge: the usual stuff of humanity. Ptolemy's epicycles grown like kudzu under the arrogant pens of Darwin, Marx, Freud, Hawkins, at al.

They discovered dark matter. Then dark energy. Then they proved entanglement and "spooky action at a distance" became not a theoretical oddity but a certainty. Then the numbers didn't work anymore, and they had to face the likelihood this isn't even the only universe—nature never did "unique," it did everything in classes—quarks, wombats, noses, galaxies—so why should there be only one universe?

So the idea of an infinite number of universes, in a hyper space-time, in multiple dimensions you couldn't even detect except through theory, and so could never check experimentally, became rational, inevitable, and all of physics suddenly became a huge, aimless bullshit session in a frat house for math nerds. And all the questions—the big philosophical questions—every single one (he looked wonderingly into Sasha's eyes) were suddenly open again. Nothing was certain. And amid the proliferating doubts, a strange light stood blinking on the horizon. Unpredicted. A shock.

You don't know anything. Anything at all.

And who would have thought that doubt's most

unexpected gift would be, of all things (he said, in a childlike voice), hope?

She looked at him with mocking tenderness.

—You've no choice, after all (she said), but to believe.

—My mother gave me ice for teething in the Pennsylvania woods, she said. You remember. We lived in a shack without windows or heat, the owls blew in on October nights and stayed till the long spring rains. My closest friend was a corn husk doll. I never saw the inside of a school till I was ten. I've always envied the Amish their buggies.

Sasha spoke calmly within earshot of her elder sister.

—You did not, they did not, owls! we did not, you little liar! her sister fairly exploding. You'd think she was on Facebook, she's such a liar, a mocking liar, a brazen liar! Give your avatar a rest, I never heard such cruddy crap!

—Don't I have a right to lie, Sasha snapped back. What's the Bill of Rights for, anyway?

—What I have to put up with! We grew up in California where the effortlessly lunatic grow on apricot trees between Salinas and Monterey and get shipped east in corroded Greyhounds, where Nixon was king and Reagan was God, and people live on pot and acid when they run out of meth and ecstasy, they forget their future and invent their past out of IT shares and suspended websites, and memory is an abandoned coastal bunker taking potshots at private drones, and liars and serial murderers and fat people march in regiments demanding their rights down the bay-washed streets of Santa Cruz, atheist college town of the sacred cross.

Her sister's shocked silence had lasted less than the time it took to lose his eye's twinkle. They had at it. Ah well. The sisters were as sisters were. He knew enough to take no side in their spats. Speaking officially. He never knew how they would conclude, stiletto stares, torrents of tears, curtains of silence, love feasts. They eventually fell unconscious even after the longest, bitterest day, waking up the next morning as if nothing whatever had happened.

—Malarkey, he said under his breath and repeated it several times. He liked how it felt in his mouth. And the sisters were shrieking too loudly to hear him.

But they are. As earnest as a trapeze act unfolding tiger-like in the upper glooms of the great tent. Where even the loudest searchlight was never known to reach, Then down in great low-sweeping arcs they soar. As though there were no safety nets in the world. But only each other's arms.

—That's the way it's supposed to be; right, children? I thought so! So, who among you will play the parents? Temporarily, of course, you can be children later, we'll rotate for a few generations, then collapse, dizzy and laughing, over the living room floor. Well, that was fun, let's do it again! They call it a journey, I call it a trip. Let's get high, then down and dirty, and whirl whirl whirl! Shoot me out of a barrel toward a bald, blue sky! I'll land on a pile of peach blossoms, I will, and sleep buried in petals till the autumn and the last oak leaves have sunk into Ellen's River. My mouth will be sealed with a coin made of ice, and a doe will lick it, the tears making it salty, till it startles us both with the quick, snuffy abrasion of its nose. As it snuffles through the soft wet matt of moss and snails and dewy weeds, rotting leaves and tangled little roots in the mud. Like a little wet kiss, the faintest little wet kiss I can remember. Then it will flee.

And your hands will be covered with worms, pink and white, as the evening gathers the ornaments in the old forgotten library and the windowpanes turn pale with gossip. The moon walking back and forth in the garden.

—"Don't fool yourself!" the old duffer said. And why not? There's nothing you can do about it. Say you've got the Alzheimer's gene, for which there is still no cure, no treatment really except drinking a gallon of coffee every day for the rest of your life, and good luck with the heeby-jeebies, thus warding off total dementia for one or two hyper-caffeinated decades. Why be told? Who wants to know? The newest television program: "Who Wants To Be A Vegetable?" What's the point of gaping at such a truth? Why not spend the rest of your life in a fairyland of your own making? A breezy, flattering, baldly self-serving dream might be your only chance at contentment in this life or the next. The hell with virtue that's its own reward! The hell with love nobody returns! Unless you get your rocks off from the rush of conceit you feel when contemplating the horror of life and feeling so much superior to the rest of humanity who can't take the bitter truth. Human life is like the Alzheimer's gene: the only thing we know for sure is we won't get out alive. All of our scientific discoveries, technological marvels, medical miracles, our spectacular wealth, billionaires, trillionaires ("capitalism is the greatest wealth generator the world has ever known"), all of our godlike power—well, I can't say it seems to have had much effect on what is sometimes rather grandly called "the human condition." Even the attack of the postmodernists (remember them?) on the concept of truth has had only one definite effect: to make a narcissistic autocrat our leader. How inconsiderate! What manners! What a bunch of pretentious punks! (To be both a punk and pretentious: now that took talent!) One by one, even the postmodernists are dying. Sad but true, if you'll forgive the four-letter word. Even if it is a racist, sexist, Western, patriarchal, phallogo-centric means of exploitation and excuse for oppression invented by Dead White Males (ahem! Yes, you—the one who's reading this. Don't look away, now. By "dead white men," you mean me?). Logos is death, and death is life's king. Not its president—it has no term limits. So let's live on dreams, let's live in a big, soft windblown bubble of enchantment, a fantasy of what life might have been if our gods had been kind and wise and not what they are: rocks and wind and exploding suns and galaxies driving across space like hurricanes.

—Will you please shut up? Sasha suddenly shouted. I can't stand this!

—What? he asked. He was alarmed, perplexed. She'd never reacted like this before. Am I boring you?

—Yes, no, I wish you would!

—All right then, I'll change my tune.

—No tune! No singing! No mansplaining! Just stop!

All right, he thought, feeling slightly huffy, though he saw she had a point.

It was really wonderful to see.

The two of them stared at the strange little thing that had dropped between them as if from the sky.

Like a child that belonged to neither of them.

—The world is too peopled, it's sinking under the human horde, in a century the human adventure might be over as we heat the planet to drought, famine, summer temperatures unbearable for birds, reptiles, higher mammals, us, all because we've been so catastrophically successful, like locusts, he babbled in his armchair environmentalist way, I'm an amateur at this, what else can I do?

—Yes, we're awful enough, she said amiably. The scourge of the earth.

—What's so terrible is losing the beautiful creatures that will go down with us. Up to now Auschwitz was humanity's greatest offense, its deepest sin against God and man. But we are preparing an even greater one, and one not resulting from hatred and fear but from childishness, greed, selfishness, an assumption that the world, the universe itself, owes us everything it has and we owe it nothing in return. What is so terrible is there is nothing to stop us until the whole thing collapses. Nothing to stop us. Nothing but us. Is that enough?

—It is. It must be, she said simply. Otherwise we're lost. Maybe we are lost. No, she said pensively. I have no reason to be optimistic, but I have noticed one thing. People are sometimes terrified into doing the right thing.

—Yes! he laughed. He addressed the night

through the window above her shoulder. The powerful are crazy, indecent, cruel—they think they'll survive. They always have. They survive, succeed; they win, that is what they do. The earth is their Titanic, they're sailing it at full speed across a dark ocean, trying to beat a record that exists only in their own heads, and ignoring every rule of prudence and concern for others or themselves, drunk on power and money and pride and an optimism that is insane. That curious shape on the horizon toward which we seem to be headed, straight as an arrow and fast as a bullet? Nothing but fog. A mirage. Anyway, even if it is something more substantial—an iceberg, say—we are such clever monkeys that we'll have invented some hitherto inconceivable device—the iBergBreaker app, even now being programmed on a smartphone in a garage in Menlo Park—to save our sorry butts between now and the time we reach it. We've always survived disasters before, always stared down Armageddon, people have been predicting the end of the world since Jesus and, look, we are, remarkably, still here. Carry on, captain, full speed ahead, I want to make New York harbor by tomorrow noon.

That's why you never wanted to have a child. Why give to a world that is courting doom with a suicidal mixture of meth-mad cleverness and moral dementia, carbon emissions, the hysteria of social media, the delirium of the internet, fratricidal hatred, the rage of the robots as they clearcut most people's means of making a living, and the ever-present nuclear bomb (how quaint the age seems that only had to worry about that!)—why give such a world a hostage of your own blood? Your crazy, possibly genetically programmed hope is that we will save ourselves at the last minute, but your hopefulness goes only so far when it is in such bitter combat with the cynical number cruncher in your frontal cortex.

In any case, your child is likely to grow up to more or less despise everything you have lived for, your obsolete "values," God help you, it will have new technologies, new arts, new species invented by the score in a psychotic neighbor's closet lab, the NSA disappearing the disgruntled at the first sign of rebellion, a smirk at the president, a shrug at a rally, they will have a new culture, new language, new scientific discoveries, a universe with more dimensions than you never dreamed of, and your child will hate, or pretend to, which is quite as bad, the outdated totality of everything you represent, that is what the next generation inevitably does, that is its law, their function in the Darwin-cum-Hegelian chain, the ball and chain cum whirlpool that is modern "reality." Every child is its parents' stranger when it isn't their murderer. It is the iron rule of the modern world. The one rule every new generation honors. Much as it pretends to despise rules.

—Yes, she said with a sigh. I was waiting for you to bring that up.

They looked down again at the thing between them, and he bent down and touched it lightly with his fingertips. It looked up at him with a puzzled, unfocussed look, as if not sure just what to make of the gigantic presence towering above it.

—Even so, our executioner is beautiful.

It might be a bit much to ask. Beggars can't be choosers and dogs will be chasers, on the third rail where the sparks fly and the flustered pigeons flutter and the moochers stare homelessly amidst the shell-fire and the ruins. And all kinds of mayhem makes itself felt, you understand. Having shaken off the parka, the snow notwithstanding.

It was time for the grass on the hill to turn red under the falling sun. The clouds were pink as icing, they looked like an enormous plain of pink sand edged by a deep cold blue, smeared and shaped by wind and ocean, but a plain that was, despite everything, upside down. Sticking to the sky like a cobweb to a ceiling.

He caught his breath when he first saw it. And realized that his cynical mornings had been non-sense, a crash course in the delusions of pessimism.

What is it about words? They're so gullible when

under the spell of their own logic. His logic is impeccable so his eyes must be wrong. There are sad word-addicts who worship a fur ball of syllables called a "text" written by another lingua-drunk, in the teeth of all evidence shouting from every side that this mare's nest of vocables cannot possibly be true, no matter how often they are repeated. "It looks wrong, it sounds wrong, it should be wrong, but, because It Is Written, it must be right!" To paraphrase a certain English composer about one of his own symphonies. Religion has much to answer for. It turned upside down, and then inside out, at least one great mind: Augustine of Hippo! The very type! And then he looks back up at the sky . . .

The pages blow away across the beach. And he feels a wild hope. Perhaps just as delusive, but sweeter.

My home is elsewhere.

—I am in love with my phantoms, we have an exclusive romantic relationship, we are faithful, monogamous, I want to marry them.

—But that's ludicrous, said Sasha, almost falling from her chair with laughter. You can't marry a phantom, even a harem of them!

—And why not? he asked. That the law doesn't say I can, or may—to say nothing of that manual of absurdity, cruelty and dictatorship, the Bible— means nothing. I'm unlikely to have any followers.

Good! I want to do as I like. And be taken by others on my own terms as I accept them on theirs . . .

—(That'll be the day! she murmured.)

. . . no more, no less. I consider myself married to my phantom ladies.

—Analog pornography unto virtual polygamy! she laughed.

—I like that! It beats the real thing any day—there's far less legal fuss and no jealousy. I visit them regularly and we have long conversations about everything on our minds, in our hearts, under the stars. Our relationship is as close to perfect as any I have ever dreamed—and far closer than any I have enjoyed in that world presumptuously called "real."

She was silent at this typical instance of his tactlessness. After all, she was right there—in the so-called "real world," no phantom, and putting up with his pontifications for years, actually listening to this stuff and trying, if not always succeeding, to understand, to sympathize, to care about and love this fool. . . .

—To find my loves, all I need do is close my eyes, and there they are, a dream that is real, reality that's a dream—what more could anyone want? An orgasm is just a click away on my computer. And I am in no danger of overbreeding the earth. I feel downright virtuous. Who am I hurting? On the contrary, I am adding a happy, contented being to the cosmos—my humble self. That sounds asinine. It *is* asinine. But it's true, all the same—and it has some, if tiny, value. "The summer's flower is to the summer sweet, / Though to itself if only live and die . . ."

—It's *beyond* asinine! she said, almost fainting with laughter. Beyond absurd! It's the perfection of fatuousness, as Lytton Strachey might have put it. I always wondered why you didn't touch me for so long. I thought you found me repulsive physically. You are the only man who never said I was beautiful. It intrigued me.

—But you are beautiful, he said. I thought you knew that and were bored with being told.

—Would you be?

—Well . . . maybe not. But then I'm not being told all the time how beautiful I am.

—Nobody, male or female, ever tires of being told how good looking they are.

—Except when that is all they're being told— when they have a brain that is being ignored. Ask Heddy Lamarr, the radar whizz who was saddled with having the most beautiful face in Hollywood. See, got you there. And I thought you were the feminist in this racket. Anyway, I only say such things to homely women—to be nice to them, to give them courage. Telling a beautiful woman she's beautiful is like telling the sun it is awfully bright and terribly hot. I hate being told the obvious, so I expect a beautiful woman to reply with something scathing like, "I know that, you idiot" or "Tell me something I don't know."

She shook her head sadly at him.

—Every woman likes to be told she is beautiful because even the most beautiful woman believes she is not, or that she might have been at one time but is losing it, has lost it. When she looks in a mirror, all she sees is her flaws. She feels like a fraud, with her make-up, her clothes, her jewelry—she thinks, without all the added fluff, would they still think me pretty? And she suspects, often correctly, that they would not. And why does she want to be pretty? Because she wants to be desired and loved, by someone she also loves, naturally—and she knows that, in this world, beauty is the only guarantor of desire, of love. Beauty of the body: people respect a beautiful mind, they like a beautiful spirit, they feel even a certain tenderness for a beautiful soul—but only a beautiful body makes them desire, makes them adore, makes them love, beyond all reason, beyond madness. *L'amour fou!* No woman will hate you for calling her beautiful, as long as you say it with respect, no, with reverence. If she seems to, it may be because you were tactless, though it's more likely because she is afraid to show you her joy. Because her joy would reveal to you your power. And your power frightens her. As it should, since even the best man can't resist abusing it.

You turned away from the bar. The portly man sat in a brown study a few stools away.

—It was, indeed, a delicious sensation. Her beauty, that is. None more so. Though, like all beauty, something of a mirage: it didn't always say what it seemed to. Or maybe a better word is enigma. This was the tragic flaw in all beauty. I saw hers, and I said, I love you, I want you, and I heard her beauty whisper, I love you, I want you, but it was an illusion. Unintended, of course: the woman couldn't help it. It's not her fault if she is beautiful or if her beauty affects you as it does: it makes her suffer as much as you. It draws people to her like flies, wasps, moths, cockroaches. She is forever under attack by appalling inamorati. But we can't help ourselves! Woman's beauty is nature's most exquisite trap. And what is nature but our genes, using their endless cunning to dupe us into regenerating? Which may be one of the reasons the spiritual masters of the past have so often counseled celibacy. And their more foolish epigones have feared women. Poor creatures, who have no way of knowing how their beauty destroys men's lives, and through no fault of their own—nor, in all cases, of ours. And why some men are driven to destroy them in order to be able to live at all. Though it were better in that case such men perished.

You stared at the ice in your glass.

—Always prefer ugly women, the portly man

suddenly said. When an ugly woman's face says I love you, it's speaking the truth quite helplessly. Pass a beautiful woman as you would a painting in a gallery, a statue in a museum, a tree in the woods. Enjoy her with your eyes, then pass on. If you find a single spark of desire inside you, stamp it out.

—I never meant it, it was a road accident, the air was thick with fog, I was in a hurry, I'm terribly sorry but you misread the signs, you were exceeding the speed limit, your brakes hadn't been checked since puberty, you were an accident waiting to happen, I am as innocent as the rain on the mountain road where we so unfortunately met.

—You were both of you as innocent as the rain. There was no fault, there was only the calamity.

He closed the book and gazed at her gravely.

—I don't know whether to laugh or cry, she said. You hopeless romantic!

His mouth smiled. Which looked strange since his eyes were so bleak.

A bit of a phenomenon from the old country, a metaphysical fairy tale, hopes unfulfilled, death between potshots at the closing barn door, a kiss against the air, a cuddle in a freshly made haystack, dry and tawny and smelling of autumn. Where he never thought the two of them would end up. And now they woke with dew on their lips. And of course they both didn't, since she had not, at that time, liked him "that way." None of the girls did. Correction: none of the girls he had wanted, at least then. So he had to make do with the plain ones, the ones said to have "a good heart," gentle ugly duck-lings waiting sweetly forever to become swans. Then it was too late. So, in one of his several alternative destinies, he settled. It was either that or face a very lonely future. He never told her this because, after all, he didn't want to hurt her feelings. He had never "loved" her, in the romantic sense, though he felt a certain affection. And he'd been loyal in his way. His impatience with females, increasing over the years, had protected both of them. He pursued, in predictably inept fashion, a number of women, but as usual they were not attracted back. Or they were, at first, and he put them off through the barely conscious resentment and distrust he radiated. Anyway, he had been, by default, faithful. It was part of his general ridiculousness.

Though he had long sought it, and sometimes thought he had at last discovered it, he had never found love. He thought at first that this might reflect more on him than on the general condition. He had found a certain superficial pleasure in a person's company, had found liking, quite sincere, found obsession, addiction, even lust, but not "love," in the sense of valuing someone or something honestly more than one's own skin, or even one's own convenience (despite there being often the pretense, a pretense that survived not a single time the first, smallest, test), a high standard, but that was what he meant by the word "love," maybe a mother felt this for her child, but he had never been a mother, and so he couldn't honestly say, in his own experience, of his own feelings and other people's actions, he had found "love," though the dearest of many people's hopes and the sweetest of their desires, little more than a fantasy, a dream, he had found love neither in himself nor in any other human being. He had not found it anywhere. He was alone, and no one knew him and no one loved him, and he knew no one and he loved no one. Or so at least it seemed. He reminded himself, dutifully, that he could be wrong, of course, about this as well as many other things. But he hadn't seen much evidence for it, in this particular case. What he could do, what he did do, was pretend to love and to be loved. And could, without loving anyone, be more or less forbearing toward his fellow shadows temporarily detached from the wall of darkness that seemed perpetually to surround him.

It could have been a lifetime between the screed and the admonition, the command and the oath. Your followers were lined up like soldiers on a ridge gazing down at the ignorant city, the horses neighing as they slip on rocks wet with dew, the dawn treacherously beautiful and cool, as if carrying, clutched in its hand, the message that will never reach you: Stop. Do not attack. We have surrendered, the war is over. And they descend silently to wreak a pointless destruction.

It could be like that. Or it might be briefer, a

sojourn over a weekend or no longer than a summer of one's youth. Remember that? It feels like yesterday. But it was a lifetime ago. It might be a gentler doom, more quiet, discreet, causing damage to only two people, bruised and aching and left for dead on the indifferent battlefield of love, cruelest of tyrants, your gauntlets bloody, your banners torn and fluttering in the dust-filled wind.

After whispering this in the darkness, you remember turning over on your side, and you must have gone to sleep, for your dreams were of an extraordinary peacefulness and peopled by young, smiling women who seemed to rejoice in you, seek to please you, to, indeed, love you.

"Of course there is love, you silly fool," they seemed to say. "It is everywhere. All you need do is open your eyes. Your mind. Your stubborn heart. You sad, foolish man. We have always loved you. It was you who turned us away. We have our pride, you know. We were just waiting for you to tell us the truth of your heart—the truth that we saw so clearly, but which we needed to hear you admit. But you were always afraid . . . "

He woke, startled and wondering, his face streaming with tears. But the dream had already vanished in the morning light. As dreams will. Those spectres.

•   •   •

—And what about you?

She turned from the doorway to the summer-house and presented him with a frank yet as always opaque pair of eyes. It was hard to believe there was really nothing there. Yet that is what he often felt when staring into another person's, a woman's, eyes: the glossy sheen of moisture, the vein-flecked white, the complex network of radiations of the iris, the dark, flexing pupil, and around the eye the lip-like opening, with its little pouty pinhole for tears to spill from, traced by eyelashes, dark and long. With the soft, smooth skin around the eye, pink and white and delicately shadowy, and the noble arch of eyebrow above, like a portal to love. And inside the eye, the sensation of endless depths, of borderless continents to explore, of a past rich with drama and promise, of a future full of longing, of seas extending beyond the infinite, and infinitely receding, horizons, worlds on worlds, the alternate universe that is every woman. And yet seeing, in a terrible, cruel, indubitable flash of insight, that there was in fact nothing there at all. And once he had seen that he could never shake the thought that there was nothing inside human beings but vacancy, and he could not take love, women, himself, life, the world, seriously again. It was all a monstrous hoax, a joke, and a very bad one at that: a joke without either humor or wit, yet one that succeeded in making a fool of him over and over again, until his life seemed nothing more than a long exercise in humiliation.

He never told her that. But he did not move closer to her where they both stood in the summerhouse. He did not take her in his arms. He did not kiss her. He did not touch her. He simply looked at her.

—What is it? she asked.

—Nothing, he replied. He felt a sudden spasm of disgust. I'm sorry, I have to go. And he left the summerhouse, walked across the garden and left by the broken gate, without looking back or promising to contact her again.

A short spell of heaven. (Which may be worse than never knowing heaven at all. Better never to have known it than have it snatched from you in the act of taking it. Like knocking a canteen full of cold water from the lips of a man who is dying of thirst.)

A spell of heaven, nevertheless. Even then, it could come over him almost too quick to catch. Like a flying fish, sparkling and wet between the swimmer and the sun. Almost grazing him. A pleasant little shock. A reminder, just in case. So he never despaired on those days on which he witnessed the rising of the sun. Or moved across a landscape in the early morning. Whatever the weather. By train, bus, car, plane, bike, or his skinny, shapeless legs. The comfort he always felt when moving across the

world with its vast, chaotic yet curiously ordered ar-
ray—each unique yet not entirely so, in a strange yet
homey, grotesque yet comforting, clutter and tangle
of infinitely individual yet ever familiar, like human
faces, natural and manmade things, jumbled and
scattered, excitable yet placid, small and big, heavy
and light, reassuringly sane and thrillingly excitable,
boxy, round, ovaline, multifaceted, like great toys
tossed across the land, with mountains lying like
great sleeping hounds, their breath rising like steam
in the chilly morning, the sea in the distance like an
enormous fallen mirror reflecting the moon and
stars staring down, as fascinated as Narcissus and
longing for the beauty they see there, not knowing
it is their own, the clouds in the sky like a carefully
painted ceiling meant to represent the sky—but it is
the sky, and this, around us, is the world.

It was the portly man again.

—The gods make us suffer so we will make better music. Make us sing the more sweetly, like cas-
trated choir boys. It's a reward of some kind, I suppose. I just wish they paid better wages.

It's so still outside today, you can almost hear the
grass growing. Though there is no grass for miles.
On the bottom landing there's a broken rocking
horse. Its legs are stiff against the blades. Its face is a
surprised smile, its mane is a leaping fire. It is racing,
racing in a panic across time. No one knows why it

is broken, but no child touches it. The only child to ever ride it was thrown off, and broke his neck. He's paralyzed from the neck down and unable to speak, though his eyes are startlingly alive. We should burn it, his parents keep saying. It's jinxed. But they can't bring themselves to do it. So it stands on the bottom landing among other junk and castoffs: a pair of red snow boots, a column of broken china, three delicate blue cups without saucers, a pile of half-decayed planks studded with nails, a crystal vase from the Gilded Age, a Raggedy Ann doll, a miniature zoo, a dried jellyfish, a cake made of angel wings, an ax made of iron and roses, a jade kiss, a goddess's eye, an ivory cornet, a golden drum, and hidden in a corner under a veil of spider webs, an ancient glass violin. And there it races in silence and darkness toward a goal it never reaches, dreaming of horses. . . .

The tang. A sweetness half sour, half bitter. As of the past, that promise of the future. Because the present does not exist. It flees even its naming.

—History, my boy, is the only immortality. It keeps the small, low flame alive, even as the barbarous present invades the city with its shrill cries and burns it to the ground in its festivals of brutality, its dance of joy among the ruins, not knowing that it itself only exists in a moment of immense polyphony and an eternity of memory as it flames through the hot needle's eye of the present. Gone!

See? Sometimes I think the world is no more than an archive of the moments imprinting it, like the tiny feet of hordes of children. It hears everything and understands nothing. But it never forgets. It's a great elephant, quiet and calm, walking through the darkness past the night's torches, its tusks gleaming; occasionally its huge ears flap somnolently, and it raises its trunk and trumpets out of sheer, irresistible high spirits. "I am alive!" it shouts out. "I see the light of the sun, I hear the wind in the trees, I taste sweet fruit, I smell the odors of narcissi and lilacs, I feel the air around my ears, I feel the earth under my feet, I carry everything on my back, and I forget nothing, not the smallest fly that ever lived, not the smallest worm lost in the mud—the world glows forever in my mind. I carry you all, the living and the dead, you are safe with me."

The portly man sighed and took a quaff from his mug.

—It has no fear, for what has an elephant to fear? Aside from us, of course. It ambles along on its great haunches, grand and gray, wrinkled with age, old as time. Older—hell, it made time! It walks through the halls of time and space like a king.

Pity had been a rich source of contentment for him. If it didn't come at too high a price.

—But how can you say that? Her voice was mildly scolding.

161

She rarely spoke to him now, and never saw him. It took him an absurdly long time to take the hint. He was forever making excuses for her. He couldn't help himself. He insisted on loving her; it was his form of pity. He was proving it was possible to love without needing to be loved back. It was his form of heroism. Sometimes he felt like a fool and then took no pity on himself. He even hated her for humiliating him. But then he realized she wasn't in fact "humiliating" him, that no one could humiliate him; his feeling of humiliation was something he did to himself. Coldness of heart is the norm; if she owed his love anything, it was respect and pity, no more. She didn't have to love him back; that was a miracle one can hope for but not demand. The lover, even unloved, knows certain hallucinatory joys, even in that lonely idolatry of another human being, that the one who doesn't love does not, will never know, a drunkenness of the spirit and celebrations in the temples of being that make of existence a continual marvel, painful as that marvel may be. The lover, if he will allow himself to love, learns a wisdom barred from the loveless; the ecstatic mystics, the Sufis, the charismatics, the lunatics of God were right. Even if there is no deity, those who love God are the lucky ones, the wise ones. The moon opens her arms to you, before you the sun solemnly dances his glory. The lover is the world's secret hero, her hidden saint, her bewildered and intoxicated angel, a small god in the universal kingdom.

So she thought she heard him say one day in the backyard as the twilight silently fell around then. The sky turned deep indigo, darker than ink, and a single star broke through the west.

—You don't need to love me. Really, he said, gently. Just let me love you.

She stared at him as he disappeared into the darkness.

—But that's just what I can't do. Her voice quivered as she spoke. I won't be able to stand pitying you, I'll have to kill your love if I want to live at all. Don't you understand? Your love will strangle me. Pitying you will kill me. So I have to kill you.

But he had already vanished in the night.

The smell of the future was in the air. It had the scent of jasmine and orange blossoms, it filled his mind with dreams and hopes and solemn promises he made to himself with all the sweet seriousness of his eighteen years.

Uncanny, how the spiders spun down from the sky one afternoon, caught on threads of spider silk. Like long strings of snow falling from the summer sky. There was brightness everywhere at the time. The dawn of his setting out on life. Certain of one thing only: that his life would not be in any way like the life he had led up till now.

The sun seemed to welcome him every day that summer, every morning was like being born all over again. He sometimes felt half drunk on light and air, his heart would lift up for no reason into a confused song of gratitude for . . . what? Breathing. He fairly worshipped the sun (The Bible? You must be kidding me. But sun worship, now, that made sense!), and the clouds, and the sky, ocean and its garrulous surf, an ever-roaring benevolent storm, and then the countryside, fields and hills and pastures, woods, fragrant in spring, green-shadowy in summer, yellow copper maroon in the fall, white and steely azure, gray, ice glassy, in winter. Nature was a temple, concert hall, museum, school, church, palace, garden of infinity sequestering nameless spirits.

And he was (as everything was) a junior member of the divine hierarchy. When he walked across a field or through a wood, he felt curiously welcome. Not that the human world he knew was particularly rejecting or harsh, as demanding as it could be—so that he often felt like a failure in it. There were, or at least seemed to be, no such auditions in the surrounding natural world in which human life was, willy-nilly, embedded: even death, in the natural world, was unemphatic, the inevitable, expected silence after the singing. Nature was immortal, all powerful, cold, and true. It was certainly not that nature was always beautiful. It had its naggingly, exhaustingly

dull spots, it could be tawdry, shabby, flat, treach-
erous, malevolent. Then he would turn a corner or
look up at the sky or glance at the earth at his feet,
and a vision of grandeur or mystery or delicacy or
beauty—there with no reference to him or to any
human being, but freely offered to anyone to par-
take of, if they care to—would take his breath away.

The thereness of nature was absolutely dependable. It was one thing he could trust.

Then one day he turned his back, out of curiosity or the fear of missing something, or the irresistible command of his genes, and entered the enigma
of history. And he discovered the bottomless abyss
of the human: its cleverness, stupidity, cruelty, love,
anger, loyalty, duplicity, fathomless violence, compulsive contradictions, fascinating, vicious ugliness,
frail and suspect beauty. He sought in the human the
grandeur, beauty and wisdom he saw in nature, and
found it in art, music, poetry, philosophy, knowledge, in architecture and the building of cities, the
creation of culture, of civilization: civilization was
humanity's forest, its woodlands. And then he discovered—or rather, became, for the first time, fully
aware of—his own will, mind, individuality, his "I,"
and he celebrated the self he had discovered and
was helping to shape, and vowed to himself to bring
whatever of beauty and goodness and truth into the

world that he could, as he understood them and as his understanding deepened: this he would press insistently on the world, these would be the terms of his conquest. And he felt himself to be a conqueror, he would mold his world into his vision of these things.

—But what if the world has its own ideas? What if it resists? she asked him, all smiling skepticism toward his unwitting (she really did believe it was, rather touchingly, unconscious) megalomania.

—Exactly, he said, with a deep sigh.

For he had forgotten: a woman might be a resistance to his great plans. He had forgotten to include that in his calculations.

He didn't know then that he had been peaking with happiness, as the scientists would discover several decades later; the years to come would be a relentless decline in his ability to feel joy, until he reached, in his middle years, a hole of despair, like a pit at the center of his life, after which he would again ascend, slowly, to a second peak of contentment with life in his late old age, should he live long enough to reach it.

All he knew at the time was that he was being regularly assailed by waves of a kind of dizzy hope and half-drunken joyfulness, for reasons he couldn't fathom and at the same time couldn't deny; they seemed as shoutingly obvious as they were inexpressible; they must seem evident and clear and unanswerable with all the logic of spring after a hard, bleak winter to anyone who shut up the chattering cerebellum for an hour and opened those dim pennies his eyes, and those flaps he called ears, drank down the sunlight in great gulps, took a draft of the day's fragrance or just tasted the air on his skin—he was, he felt himself, immediately, overwhelmingly, himself, to be, and to be surrounded by, immersed and drowning, in the loveliest way possible, in the sublime and beautiful and dark and terrible and luminous and brilliant and sultry and ambiguous and demanding and death-haunted and glorious and perilous, the terrible wonder and miracle of being alive.

And when that December he heard of the murder of twenty children in a New England town by a young man close to his own age, he sat alone in his room and suddenly broke down, crying.

The world was beautiful, terrible—brutal, generous, cruel, enchanting, filthy, sublime, ingenious, insane, heartless, wise. A horrible knot of paradoxes, senseless. And his joy vanished. It seemed based on a mistake, a delusion of the moment, naïve, immature.

But, being eighteen still, he soon forgot the horrors of the day and was once again struck, again and again, as by a hammer, with unasked-for joy, little ecstatic fever storms that came at unexpected moments (a view of a forest glade from a car window, a slant of light on an alley wall, a motion in the clouds in a winter sky, a thread of birdsong in early morning, a whiff of flowers in spring, of over-ripe tropical fruit—mangoes, papayas—in late summer, in a city street), and feelings of gratitude and joy moved across him like waves in a restless sea. And his days were once again a long hallelujah just waiting to break through the tedium of dailiness, high school, chores.

—My best friend's sister once even accused me of being on drugs, but I wasn't. My body sang out at times like an angel choir of the faith. The voix mystères des Bulgars have nothing on me!

—Faith in what? she asked, coolly, not unkindly.

—In life, he shrugged. The world. Everything. It doesn't matter what. He paused and thought for a moment. I couldn't choose not to believe. Yes, that's it. I really had no choice. And I didn't really want one. I was a bone in the mouth of a very happy puppy.

Because life was joy before becoming pain. Before the egrets settled on the bountiful nests of the south and flexed their wings above the crowd. There was such a stillness then, such a sigh. The male nodded his beak with elegant reserve, and the female shyly tucked her head under her wing; it was so sweet, and you crept away silently so as not to disturb them in the delicate task they were in the middle of.

Three weeks later, a clutch of egretlings shrieked tinily in the nest under the protective, blank-eyed mother, and the great male went proudly hunting up food for the family.

Not so painful after all, then, just part of the necessary wheel turning, turning on the world's axle. It creaks as it turns, squeals, sometimes screams, please, stop, I'll tell you everything, but nothing stops it because nothing started it, it goes on and on, unrelenting. Like a handful of water raised to a pair of beautiful lips.

And you never even knew you were being kissed.

Though that means nothing. The world has the golden heart of a whore, and being good liberals and nice, tolerant people, you celebrate it. Though what if you were wrong. What if the Catholics have been right all along? What if the Republicans have been right? That's enough to curl your toes. But we won't go there, shall we.

And yet, why not? What kind of cowardice is that? What are you afraid of? Being ostracized by your liberal friends? If they drop you for a principle, they were poison and a snake. A friend never lets a mere idea, however moral or noble, however right, wall up between you like an ox skin mangy with fleas and sparkling with caviar and stolen pearls, those frozen oyster's tears. A friend will wrap himself in its pelt and hug you ever closer to his heart because of the feral distance between your minds.

The cries of the hunter volley across the plateau when he seizes the deer's rack of mud-smeared antlers and twists its neck down to the snow. His victory is a bitterness to the earth. His success is the tolling of a bell for the world, where his feet lay waste cities and his shoulders cut through continents of cloudbanks and his eye challenges the sun. Terrible is his birth out of the earth's loins. His howls echo down the halls of the world and not a sound responds. His teeth crush mountains and the globe shakes in his hand like a rattle. Paul Bunyan redux.

No, an idea will never separate you. The vaults of your ambition can't contain your pride. There's nobody out there to love you. You lurch toward endless consummations. Your paradise is an endless fall.

But he lacked the courage and character for such a purple patch. To say nothing of the energy. And his intelligence had long been a kind of dubious glue holding together the warring provinces of his mind, which, even at that time, were barely on speaking terms with one another. He had often felt like a dyspeptic parliament, of factions ever quarrelling, often at the point of civil war. Internecine strife was a favorite phrase during those years. Dealing with the rest of the world was just not going to happen. Let it go to perdition in its own way, he had a hard enough time keeping food on his table.

The squabbling youngsters at the bottom of the wall lit fires that lasted far into the night. Their smartphones chattered at each other and sent salvoes of texts and compromising pictures across a fiber-optic-veined globe that would long outlast the death of the analog, sailing across the stillness of space in great walls of agitated waves, cruel revelations and bad jokes, hate speech and death threats, pompous screeds and silly ringtones, that would keep the stars company and bewilder the civilizations of the future. How could such a clever species have been such crazy fools? And they would look at each other, shake their heads and rumble their bellies with laughter.

As the stars shone down on the barrel of the rifle and the prayer rug's crimson stain.

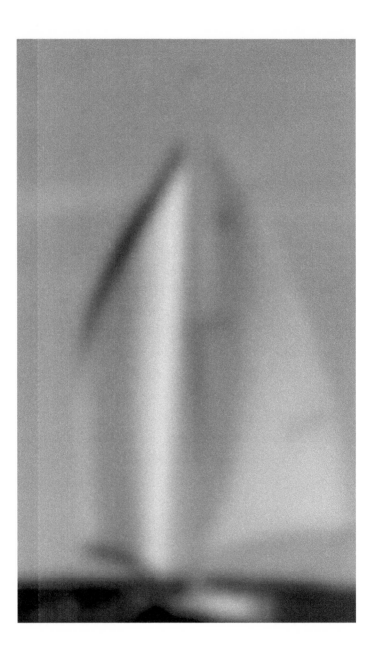

Free at last. At last . . .

That was the echo he heard before setting out on his next quest. The last illusion, pleasant as it was. Though who could say, perhaps it wasn't an illusion at all. Perhaps it was the real thing. Finally.

Or, on the other hand, not even the last illusion.

A certain poignancy was in the air, a sad-sweet, bitter-tart flavor that made all things dim, like a memory at the edge of the last forgetting. It would have been almost pleasant if he'd been able to indulge it, but his hectic schedule and the ludicrous demands of job and relationships gave him no peace; responsibility killed his tranquility with its thousand tiny cuts. How he loathed it! Yet he hated above everything else to disappoint people—a foolish weakness, but there it was. Any fool held the ax over his head, any weakling held his pity in his hand like a lash. He couldn't say no to even the mere threatening of another person's pain. And they had no pity for him. So the lash sang in the morning air with the dependability of sunrise and the exquisite pain of a rooster crowing obsessively in his ear, "Be nice! Be good!"

—I can hear them shouting still, he said. Goodness is an exquisite little tyrant.

—Do you mean me? she asked, with an innocent raising of her two magnificent eyes.

—Women burn with virtue, he said, they would heave their lover like a log onto the pyre of goodness without hesitating if it would increase by the width of a hair their sense of righteousness, their monstrous moral pride—what, after all, is a lover for, he said, with a smile. Why are you looking so shocked?

—I never realized how much you hated us.

—But I don't hate you, he said. Why do you think I'm here?

—Because you pity us. You hate us and you pity us.

He gave that some thought.

—You're forgetting something. I hate you. And I pity you. And I desire you.

—And that, she said in triumph, is a glue that will never dissolve.

Called adulthood, if I remember correctly, that curious fraud, that Gordian knot. Though not to be cut through so easily.

Quondam. Where did that come from? The love affair that never was. Except in his adolescent mind.

•   •   •

Dewpoint. Tears. Sickness of the eye. Cotton-wool spots and the ora serrata. The zonules of Zinn. No relation to the radical historian fashionable among the young at the time. Apparitions along the wire past the trench near Hamel. A corporal hung out to dry in the searing August sun. The flies doing their job. The stench of a dead horse among the marigolds. The hallucination of a whistle shrilling down the line, another, then another, fading into the distance like fleeing birds. What are they fleeing? The smell of battle, mud, shit, piss, decaying bodies. It wakes you up in the morning better than coffee. A sign from the masters that the war is still going on and no one will let the dead be dishonored by any thoughts of peace, I mean, surrender. And so the war must last forever, logically considered, since peace is surrender, and surrender is dishonor, not for the living, but for the dead, and no one has the gall to fail them. The balls to fail them. To admit you were defeated the moment you began. The long battle of your time. The endless war.

—Are you listening? he asked.

But she must have fallen asleep. The sunlight crept up her arm toward the tangled hair over her face.

So: be careless and free. Not quite! By being careless, one will soon be the opposite of free. But be free, for all that. A book of wise sayings half hidden in flowery digressions. Don't give a rhino's rump for fame, power, wealth, love, authority, status, reputation, family, friends; give a damn for freedom and the dreams of the senses, the smell of the morning, the slant of light in the late afternoon, the cool wind off the sea, the gathering of shadows in the woods in the evening, the silent twilight and the first star, the bone-white moon in the black sky. A feeling light as a breath. An idea dissipating like a wisp of cigarette smoke.

Keep those ideas open—they have a bad habit of flinging shut like a gate in a gale. Locking you in. But that is a spiritual crime, a philosophical sin: caging the mind with an idea. For every lock of an idea, seek the key of a sensation. Trust only a word you can smell, the winters of its past hang on it like the rags of a favorite glove, the smell of wood burning in the fireplace, or of your mother's perfume when she kissed you before leaving for the evening. Hold it in your hand like a pebble, a talisman. Breathe it deep, secretly. Look for it again among the trees. Then hide it. It is our secret.

He watched her sleeping. She slept on.

Her glorious, coal-black hair. That perfect, sculpted profile. Her heart cold as a pocketful of ice. You'd think he did hate her, so hard and unblinking was her love. If love is the word for it. The obsession of a survivor with its image. In whose depths a hand may fall, all the way down to the streambed of decaying leaves. That flying carpet that teems with life. The smell of rot is the smell of life. Its eternal churn. If not technically eternal, as close as one is likely to see. I am. We are. You are. Ocean crashing along the writhing, whiplash coasts, a labyrinth coiled into Ariadne's thread. Like the path from her lips to her heart. Never to be seen again. How in love we were with romantic superlatives! You have taken everything else away from me, at least leave me that. A certain melodramatic extravagance, a sentimental tenderness, a naïve tear and forlorn smile. Weakness itself (as the great Dane put it) become a force.

He said, but she was no longer listening. You should have realized all along that this would be the plot.

Let the light man levitate at will. The psychologists had criticized him for his flying dreams, but they gave him such pleasure, such loony joy, that he despised their reasons, nothing that gave such pleasure and that hurt no one (how could a dream hurt anyone, even the dreamer?), such a feeling could not possibly be wrong. And even if it were: tant pis! No one should spurn any taste of paradise offered on this earth, it may be the only taste of it you'll ever have; it's one of the handful of reasons for being alive, to be caught up and caressed for a moment in bliss, it's enough to make you fall in love, head over heels, with life all over again and forget every lie and false promise it ever made you. No words can capture it, did you ever notice that? Not mine, not yours, not the words of Shakespeare or God. Maybe nothing can, not even art at its most hypnotic or music at its most time-annihilating. At best they capture the shadow of bliss, but never its intoxicating body. It has no shadow, it has no illusion (words are the illusions, not what they strive, falteringly, to mean: being tyrants, they try to convince us that, if they are not entirely real (and there's the trap: even words know that words are not, cannot be, completely real: they are centaurs of reality and illusion), that nothing else is allowed to be either, because words taint everything. Put words in their place: they are your servants, you are not theirs—except when you forget yourselves, out of laziness or ignorance or cowardice, and let them become your masters).

A Nietzschean capable of love. That is what he wanted to become. Not a hydra of egotism, but a lover of the world. And of its creator, its god. (Or, if he must become a hydra, he wanted it to be: a loving hydra.)

—Have I gone over the top again? he asked in a whisper.

But Sasha was still sleeping.

Pascal was suddenly frightened. She hadn't moved in so long—maybe she was dead?

Alarmed, he pressed his fingers against the side of her throat (it was soft and still warm) and felt the quiet pulsing of her blood. He gasped (he had been holding his breath) and tears came to his eyes: he had for a moment been afraid she had died, lying near him, in the summer afternoon.

He curled up next to her and soon drifted back to sleep, hoping to dream again of flying.

If only you could be good. It always seems beyond you. Rubbernecking the violent end of many a grand hope or obstreperous folly. Because you could, for no other reason, it seemed at the time. What sometimes seemed the nullity of the human, the vastness of the ignorance built in to the smooth-skinned simian one was. The trick was to have an intelligent back. Something out of Watteau. Too many backs were simply blank. Women were good at the pretense—the off-shoulder T was subtle as a wink seen from the back row of a bus, though it fooled no one, not even themselves, in the end.

Nothing like a good illusion to set one up in the morning. Good as a toad before breakfast. Even though you always said it was better to believe something, we never said it was necessary to believe somebody. It would have embarrassed the cynics among us.

Better to say nothing in front of them. One mustn't betray them. They'll get the bad news soon enough. What bad news, you say? Why, the unwelcome discovery that the darkness of their thoughts is even more foolish than their previous innocence. There is more wisdom in a spoonful of innocence than in all the cynic's wisdom—which, after all, is little more than an excuse for cowardice after getting hurt a few times while trying, and failing, to break a stallion.

Have a bit of courage. Hope. Faith. The gods are strangely fond of you even when you neither love yourself nor believe in them. Their laughter is full of tenderness. It echoes through the palace and flies out the casements like doves carrying messages into the night; every galaxy, every gravity wave in space-time, is an echo, fading as long as the sound of the big bang, of the gods' affectionate laughter.

He said, and she smiled, sleeping. (Oh, he thought, are you really listening, then, even in your sleep?)

It lacked, let's say, a certain heroism. The lab spoon resting on the dusty lab table, the retorts lined up in short rows between the microscopes, the pipeds arranged like little cigars. The chemical of Amberley and the rank mud of Catrina, Biloxie,

Transmarin, in the late fall, just before the frosts locked the ground. An atom of doubt and maybe we will not even notice. The trail of slime on the windowsill. The coil of shell on the wet cement. The ceaseless wind off the lake. Even in summer it's cold where you come from. Attributes, characteristics, and other ailments that result from combining flesh with time. Though only ideas were real; dirt hid the roots. Nature was the face of God; you couldn't bear to look it in the eye. It was like a mirror molded inside the dome of the Pantheon, the sun piercing the center. Being human, you had a lot to learn. And even the "much that you learned" turned out, in the end, to be wrong. And you never even found it out. There's injustice for you. Could it be said you've really learned anything at all? Do you understand? No, it's all right, I didn't think so. Well, we'll have to start again from the beginning.

—Are you still there? he asked.

But she didn't answer. Perhaps she had run away, as they all did in the end. Sensible girl.

He felt his forehead for the lines. I'm really too intense, it upsets people. Ah, but it's my poor shadow of being, my little crumb of joy. The god appears, like the aura before an epileptic's fit. What if the divine appears only in the chinks of what we like to call "reality" (a mid-afternoon café, dusty sunlight against the chipped tiles, last decade's pop hits in the background, the smell of coffee, sliced cold cuts), the slippages between the plates, fevers, flaws, the spaces and silences carved out, thumbed and shaped, like clay and pastry dough, between those delicate hazards called words, hapless children of the human brain? The lightning cracks the darkness between thunderheads, and through the crack, violent, brief as a blink, a blink, paradoxically, not of darkness but of brilliance, the divine seeps into the world, like a drop of wine, tears, blood. And you drink, your thirst assuaged for half an hour.

—Look into the eyes of your neighbor and you will see the world. Listen to the voice of your neighbor and you will hear the sea. Hold the hand of your neighbor and you will touch the sun. Are you listening yet? he asked

No answer.

—Of course, I may be wrong, but in this case I think I may be right. Who knows, in the end? We have nothing to go on but belief. As in: I believe you are listening to me.

Still no answer.

The sound of a dripping faucet. Or is it a clock?

Here there is a gap in the manuscript, somewhere between the lost coast of Mauretania and the slot canyons of Utah.

It's clear from the photographs they had no idea where they were headed. Yet not a single face was without interest, even a kind of beauty. He lingered over them late into the evening. Where have they all gone, these people? They have gone into the photographs. Into his eyes, then into his brain . . .

She felt so much better afterward. He had been a burden, with his emotional outbursts, his clinginess, his manipulative sweetness, his "love." There's no burden like somebody else's love. It's bad enough to love without having it returned, though that's the most common form it takes. But to be loved without returning it is also intolerable, ultimately, if not immediately as painful: no one ever committed suicide because they were loved by someone they didn't love back. Or had they? (Item for internet research.)

She almost hated him, though she had to admit her ego was flattered. After all, he wasn't a bad catch: he had a certain reputation, and the idea that this small-town celebrity had fallen for her gratified her vanity. Her heart was left cold. And she felt no physical attraction. In fact, she disliked his smell. That was what most repulsed her. He was not aggressively ugly, kind of like a chow; he was intelligent, kind, generous, playful, even witty sometimes. He was dependable, loyal, and he seemed to love her truly, for herself: he admired her accomplishments without resentment or jealousy, he liked her intelligence, she didn't have to play dumb around him, and he would always be on her side; she felt that, and she felt actual guilt that she couldn't return his affection. He deserved better. But he stank. And not that pungent, sweaty, sexy-foul smell of men's locker rooms she got a whiff of whenever she passed one with the door open. She could not stand sitting next to him for any length of time. The odor diffusing from him was just too disgusting, like a barrel of bad oysters. And when he opened his mouth to tell her how much he loved her—well, she thought she might faint. And she could see in his eyes he thought she was nearly fainting from love, desire, longing—he looked positively stupid with gratitude. She almost laughed in his face. Had nobody ever told him? What were mothers for but to deal in unpleasant truths to protect their precious male offspring from the opposite sex's unforgiving contempt? What a curse it was for him, and he didn't even know! She almost felt sorry for him. But she wouldn't sleep with him for the world. They had finally broken off, and she felt the monkey, with his puzzled, hurt eyes and his mangy stench rise away from her, like a shadow against the sun.

—So they tell me. He wept for days, every twilight, because he had lost her. Of course, he had never had her, but that was no comfort. The driveway was littered with maple leaves, like little crimson gloves, glistening in the rain. Somewhere east of here it was snowing.

He detested the philosophical materialism of his age, though he saw no way out of it. Something so detestable, that offends him at almost every level, cannot be true. Yet what if it were? Why must reality respect anyone's feelings? Why not despise reality as much as it despises him? If "materialism" (which drove behind every impotent gesture toward any kind of ideal, philosophical or religious) were true, human life seemed little more than a mutually agreed upon deception, a practical joke human beings played on each other (on themselves) with the help of a random universe, without any meaning or point but to keep the game going for as long as possible, a test of heroism without reward, in a dingy little hellhole called planet Earth. The joke had several alternative punch lines, "romantic love' being only one of them ("religion," "science," "philosophy," "patriotism," "morality," "family," "money," "power," "art" being some of the juiciest of them).

But in the end he couldn't call them lies, life and love, despite all the evidence: his romantic heart cried out against the roar of atoms and quanta: "There is nothing more precious than life, however painful, and the most precious thing in life is love, however betrayed. The lover is more holy than the beloved. The broken heart is exalted, a relict in the chapels of paradise, worshipped by spirits, spectres, angels."

Yet what were these "spirits, spectres, angels" his heart spoke of? Or was he just being driven back to childhood, blind hope, blissful ignorance and Sunday school? His society's noisy "golden lie"?

Must the divine exist, to save the wrecked world, though the only evidence for its existence was the ache of the soul and the heart's longing? That was the only sign you had. Your hunger proves the existence of food, your thirst the existence of water: if you had not known them, you could hardly desire them now. You have known them because you needed them. You cannot exist without them, therefore, in principle (though perhaps not right here and now, where you are crawling through the middle of a desert, where you woke after your plane crashed and you were almost violently born) they exist. Your existence proves their existence.

Does your longing for a universal sense of meaning and love thus prove their existence? Even if such things do not in fact exist, does that mean one must not choose the illusion that they do? Why not, if they make you happier and more content? Just because it offends someone who thinks he is wiser? But why should you respect such people? They do not respect you. You crush them between two thoughts and choose the way that pleases you. Because their contentment is nothing to you—and yours, let's face it, is everything.

If the truth destroys the spirit, why not reject it for an illusion that makes you dance across the night, makes you fall in love with it, with life; that makes you kinder toward your fellows, makes you forgive everything that ever made you suffer?

Dostoyevsky's Stavrogin claimed that, if he had to choose between the truth and Christ, he would choose Christ.

—And look what happened to him, said Sasha. He raped a child and hanged himself. Not my favorite role model.

—The truth has its place for practical purposes, he said, raving. In the operating room you don't want happy illusions.

And when your pride gets a little hungry, your ego impatient with these childish ways, you can snack on a bitter truth now and again and feel superior, sneering at your fate.

Such hope in such despair being its own reward.

•   •   •

But it doesn't anymore. (Doesn't what? she asked.) Happen as it used to. I remember you smiling at me. I remember me smiling at you. (I can't say I remember either of those things. Or if they happened, they were pure reflexes. They were social smiles, meant to ward off hostility, to express harmlessness and peaceful intentions. They had no expressive meaning or intention whatsoever.) That isn't what I remember. (You can't trust memories. They all lie.) Not always and not everywhere. (Where emotions are involved, almost always.) Then how am I to be so sure that what you say you remember is accurate either? If I have to choose between your memory and mine, thanks, but I think I'll choose mine. First of all, because it's more beautiful. (To you.) True: more beautiful to me. (And I choose mine because it seems more likely to be true.) No, because it's meaner, and you think the meaner the thought, the more honest, the truer. Sometimes I'm afraid of you, you have a cruel streak, or maybe it's just anger, and you're looking for a reason, any reason, to fight. (You're wrong. I don't want to fight you, you want to fight me, everything you say is meant to provoke me. Everything you say is an attack. All you want to do is win.) No, no, no, I don't accept your terms in this debate. (You're trying to impose your meaning on me. I won't have it!) I'm not trying to impose anything on you, I'm just trying to express what I feel and understand. (You won't let this go, you're being insistent and disrespectful.) No, I'm just not letting you win, I'm standing up to you and not letting you bully me. (You don't hear what I'm saying! Stop this!) Stop what? Stop speaking? I can't, I won't. Don't order me. (Don't order me! You're being selfish and childish in trying to impose your ideas and feelings on me.) I am not, that's not what this is about. Why are we fighting? I don't understand this, I don't understand you. Why are you behaving like this? (What about the word stop do you not understand? You're being violent in your insistence. I want no more communication from you. I will not listen. If you communicate with me again I will seek recourse to stronger action.) Like what? Like who? Like when?

A lot more money. Than you had at the time. And boy did you need it. As anybody would in your position. But you didn't know how to get it. There were the banks of course, "because that's where the money is"—at least most of it. But that took a skill set you didn't have the mastery of. Yet. And you might get caught. Twenty years in Vacaville is no joke. I hear the beds are pressed together like sardines, the wards stink of dry sweat and piss, they're loud, they never turn off the lights, you may wake up once too often with somebody else's dick in your mouth and if you don't make like you're loving every moment of it, you could end up dead before your time, and if you try to make any complaints about any of this, they put you in the hole, solitary, for weeks.

—Hell, caught? You might get shot. Security is trigger-happy since 9/11.

—There's always drugs, of course. Making the connection can be tough. Don't want to look like you're mooching on anybody's territory. That also can be fatal.

—What else? Pickpocketing? Takes practice, a lot of, and time is one thing we ain't got.

—Mugging drunken techies on the way home from the clubs after 2 a.m.? Prob is they all try to look like teens, with their dippy convict pants and stupid baseball caps stuck on backwards—you can't tell those motherfuckers from teenybopper types, and those guys ain't got no money, not even credit cards with, like, fifty-dollar limits.

—Shit. Gonna have to peddle my ass on Polk Street.

—Your forty-year-old butt ain't gonna catch no ooga-booga, dude, you gonna have to pay them to pay you. This is called not a good return on investment.

—Man! What ya gonna do? Get a fuckin' job?

—Hey, man, there be no fuckin' jobs for us, dude. And the robots comin' to take the ones they got left.

He looks at his empty hands and listens to the growl in his guts. A shadow passes, bends down and flips a coin into the hat lying like a sleeping animal beside him on the sidewalk.

Ocean. A drop of it in your palm. The smell of decaying seaweed, jellyfish, mussel beards, razor clam shells, crabs. The question of meaning never even comes up. It's too, I don't know, there for that. In your face. Whoever thinks life is meaningless has never taken a walk, alone, on a beach. Across a field. Into the woods. And simply been attentive. Look at the sky. Correction: try to look at the sky. What after all does "the sky" mean? One can only laugh, embarrassed, for the questioner. You deny our existence a meaning because you don't want it to have a meaning. Because you're afraid you won't measure up to the one you find. Because it might impose an obligation. Because your pride wants to deny any significance that exists without your explicit consent. Because there is no depth of spiritual awfulness to which your pride won't descend in an attempt to make yourselves the only value in the world. In the universe. A hubris of breathtaking scope.

—The bankruptcy of humanism, the rot of human pride, he said at last, having mulled over these issues over several drinks and a toke of hashish.

—Having kept your freshness like a rose, she said, not unsympathetically, though not even trying to keep up with him.

He chuckled. The word, she decided, was, for once, apt. It was more comfortable than a snicker, less nervous than a titter, less self-conscious than a chortle, less blatant than a guffaw, less liberally open-jawed than a plain old laugh.

—Touché, babe. But we're nowhere near enough. We need a god to save us.

—To quote your favorite philosopher, she said. Too bad he was a Nazi. (He winced; she ignored it.) And what if we can't find one?

—We'll have to invent one.

—To quote another one! she laughed, open-jawed and liberal. Philosopher that is, not Nazi.

—The old gods are dead. Nobody takes them seriously any more. The fundamentalists are the last spasm of a corpse. We need a new god.

—And what if we can't find him—her—it? And if we can't invent one?

—Then we're stuck with the slow suicide of "humanism."

—But doesn't Darwin prove life is meaningless, without purpose, random and pointless?

—Natural selection proves nothing but natural selection. Apply a little chaos theory to it, you'll see.

—And what about quantum theory?

—And fractals! Apparently random systems create patterns, shapes, order—purpose—meaning, just as simple operations, repeated ad nauseam, create extraordinary complexity: molecules, life, brains, Spem in alium, Finnegans Wake, the career of Picasso. What if the universe is a gigantic self-organizing system that aims toward ever tighter organization? Even mind? Even (gasp!) soul.

—I hate to spoil your little party, she said, with a sigh. But I have one little naughty word to disappoint you with.

—Don't tell me.

—Entropy.

—Ugh! But I have a way out.

—It better be way out.

—The second law of thermodynamics states that in every closed energy system, entropy increases; that is, all of the system's organized structures break down and all of its energy is diffused, eventually, into heat.

—I'm already yawning. Is that what that old poet meant by "Not with a bang but a whimper"?

—But there's a catch. What if the universe is not a closed energy system? If there is an infinite number of universes, then the "metaverse," which includes, or embodies, or whatever, that infinite number of universes, is therefore itself infinite, cannot be closed: it regenerates forever, world (or at least multiverse) without end. In a sense each universe can be said to be creating its own god. Just have a little faith. Imagine a rose that takes a trillion trillion years to open. We are living on one of its smallest, most delicate, youngest of its petals. Yet even we can "see" it.

—Well. Maybe you can. In your grand cosmological theory for this week. Wait another week, and it'll be shot down dead by some snarky, ambitious new astronomer, some butch femme with a mean streak and a deep desire to kick a man's butt just because he could be an astronomer for the last 3,000 years and she couldn't. She so wants a universe that no man will ever be able to understand.

He shrugged.

The prevailing winds. Off the eastern promontory. Waxing and waning at will, like the moon in its phases. The tides rising, falling. The churn of birds above the corn fields. The waste of dust behind a tractor. The smell of exhaust fumes behind a bus. People appearing and disappearing like phantoms in the fog. A meritorious deed, somewhere between courtesy and heroism. Almost ignored at the time. Forgotten, as all acts must eventually be. A million years from now, who will remember it? Not I, I promise you. I'll have too much on my hands. The

wind moveth where it listeth. We may as well follow it as anything else. Though it promises a very
meagre wage. The tents are blowing at the end of
the meadow. The ferns wave like big green hands
around them. One of the flaps is open, and a small
pale face peers out.

All because of the photographs. Or so they said.
The curious ability to capture a moment and embrace it more or less indefinitely. To capture time.
That was the golden ring. There was a kind of purity
in that face staring out at you from its little niche in
the past. Whatever awfulness it faced out of: famine,
war, revolution, hurricane. Turning at the far end of
the avenue, the distant crackling of gunfire, the random shouts. The chanting of fans in the old foot-
ball park, like the sounds of ghosts in a Roman are-
na. The ominous thumping of a helicopter poised
half a mile above the city. The thronging mobs.
And among all of that, a face frozen in black and
white on a piece of glossy paper, caught slightly off
guard, both ugly and beautiful, staring toward you,
past you, not seeing you, not even imagining you,
hardly aware of the photographer, who was only an
obscure figure behind a box and a fish-eye-looking
lens, and disappeared almost immediately into the
crowd, taking with him your splinter of afterlife.
Who'd have guessed paradise would turn out to be a
darkroom? she asked, with a little laugh, Or if we're

doing digital, not even that! The servers of the internet. A DVD. A smartphone. The cloud. A flash drive no bigger than Sasha's thumb.

No. Yes. Maybe. After joy, bitterness, because the joy had led you to believe in an illusion. There's no greater generator of illusions, you discovered to your dismay, than happiness.

—Codswollop, somebody replied. Better a happy illusion than a miserable truth, if that's the alternative. Better happiness than reality.

—But you can't live without facing it sometimes. Then it bites.

—Then bite it back.

—But what bliss it was . . . !

Which is why he remembered his childhood with such fondness: he'd had so many beautiful ideas about the future. As he lost them, one at a time—the tooth fairy, Santa Claus, Christianity, America, love, "greatness," history, philosophy, art—the compensations betrayed him as well, often at the moment of possession.

Women, too. He liked them, though they rarely returned the favor. His personality was odd, his prospects dim, he had all sorts of old-fashioned attitudes, so women would, after a moment of curiosity, place him firmly back on the shelf. Then he would become obsessed with them, and stick like glue; in one or two cases, they had to summon with the police to scare him off their doorstep. Which left him shattered and in despair. Rather than blame himself, he took it out on them, pretended to despise them: it felt better than despising himself. And decided that, in the battle of life, a shrewd but ruthless self-love was the strongest weapon.

That was the one compensation he embraced.

He had hoped for a little loving, a modest happiness, a few trustworthy friends, a dependable, if small, income, the prospect of a happy and just afterlife, a caring and loving God, etc., etc., etc. Embarrassing, childish hopes, whose biologically salutary effect may have often inspired human beings to reproduce, but that had little prospect of being realized and, when they were, no prospect of lasting. He felt himself becoming a kind of court fool of natural selection, forever trying to convince himself that life was good, that he loved life, that it was of value to be alive, even if (he thought in his darker moments) that it was not, they did not, it had no value, and that he kept living out of habit and cowardice.

She was awkwardly silent throughout his latest discourse. This troubled him. Silence did not often mean consent in her case.

Of course, he may well have gotten it completely

wrong. Knowing what she thought was, after all, as easy as listening to what she said. In other words, as difficult, and sometimes as impossible. Because so much of what came out of her mouth was like reels of barbed wire. That voice, at first so quiet, had become bright, adamant, spraying little splinters of a frantic truthfulness, a sincerity too frank to scorn, in accents of tireless rebuke. So much so that any sinking to softness, tenderness, even consideration, immediately put him on his guard: what did she want from him now? And she was, alas, one of the good ones, moral to a fault. So perhaps it was better not to know exactly what she was thinking at any given moment.

—Rectitude, where is thy gentleness?

The neonates on parade in the maternity ward. Of course, she would want to have a delivery at home. It would have been agreed to months before. How does one describe the muck-about of birth?

—Badly, sirrah, said the portly man. Pascal looked up. Night had fallen across the windows, leaving the interior lights a bourbony haze. The portly man went on: Having undergone it once myself and promptly forgotten it. The coming here even as the going hither. Naked and half-blind. The ludicrous necessity of it. To say nothing of the utter triviality that is its cause. Forthwith into the human darkness. Then out of it again. Forgiving where one can, since

no one here had been consulted beforehand. Heave-
ho, Romeo, and cheerio, in! Then heave-ho, Antonio,
and cheerio, out! Between which were several decades of forced labor for the grand panjandrums of
the era. With odd hours of recreation, even the occasional vacation, a few entertainments for consolation, usually about sods even worse off than oneself,
to take the edge off: music and art and philosophy
and science and poetry and movies and dancing and
novels, you get the picture, to keep you docile and
malleable in the manipulative fingers of the aristos
and the chromosomes. Wealth, power, fame, love,
sex, the gaudy inducements to keep your nose to the
grindstone, your attention on the task at hand, and
your gonads out of trouble. Poverty, boredom, obscurity, indifference, shame, ostracism and celibacy
the threats and common fates of any who rebelled:
they were too smart to kill you outright, it might
turn you into a hero, a martyr. One Lenin's brother
is more than enough. To say nothing of Socrates
and Christ. No: you must be made to look ridiculous: no reputation can withstand that. Destitution,
misery, contempt, impotence and frigidity were the
disciplining fears. Sweat, frustration, disappointment, worry, shock, the wall, humiliation, and death
were the universal experience—even, in the end, for
our masters, though they spent their lives pursuing
the illusion that, with just a little more money, a little

more power, they might be able to avoid them, to live, and to live happily, forever. A recent delusion of theirs is the coming of the singularity.

—Now, there's a really human life for you! the portly man continued, with a royal smack of his lugubrious lips. Of course, only a god can save us, Martin, old boy! Good God, Christopher, we can't!

—What is "the wall," you say? The wall is what stands between you and what you most desire. It is stone-gray, thick as desire is deep, and as high as your will is long. On each side it stretches as far as your lifetime. It is sometimes transparent. Just on the other side of it, there, almost within reach, is the object—she, he, it—dazzling, radiant, smiling— opening its arms to you, a breeze lifting a strand of hair—of your longing. A spectre. Against the wall all you have is your fists. They are bloody and shredded from your pounding.

You wake up in a sweat.

A pale tide. Stretching like a rumpled sheet toward a vague, cloud-banked horizon. That was how time felt then. And he was standing at the edge of the beach in a white T-shirt and a pair of tan shorts, his feet in the wave wash, staring, his mind wandering between possible futures. What shall I choose? What will be chosen for me? What will I be forced to do, to be? How many of those doors will be closed to me? Now he knew: the ones that had seemed most invitingly ajar were the ones that had been most firmly shut. The ones above all he had wanted to open. Or so he imagined.

Desire had been the trap. The world was a war of desires. He hadn't gotten what he wanted; he'd gotten what wanted him. This had been the rule of his life. What does life desire most strongly? To last in strength, beauty, youth, hope. Precisely what it is not allowed to have. The most that's allowed is to have them for a time, and then bear a child who can also enjoy the same imaginary enchantments for a time, who will then be able to have a child who . . . through creating a chain of generations who can touch, with their fingertips, the high floor of heaven at the price of regularly pressing their lips against the walls of hell. Human existence is such a ridiculous fate, the worst thing you can do to a soul is land it in the body of a man or woman; it really ought to be treated as a capital offense. Parents are murderers, the portly man declaimed. Yet we can only know the godlike spectacle of the world, its grandeur and beauty and power, to say nothing of its clever, cruel, wildly imaginative humor, all of which are often almost unbearable— well, actually they are unbearable, since they kill us in the end—by being born into it. It's as though the universe had been created by an exploding god and we were his fragments, rags of infinity blowing through the endless darkness ever since. The very biggest of big bangs. You are thus an ember of God as it slowly, over inconceivable stretches of time, millions of eons, flickers out. This gives your self-esteem a boost out of self-pity, and a certain respect for your fellow creatures: the sand crab near your foot, the gull puling overhead, the funny little girl frowning at you.

—That was me, she said, with a little cock of her head.

—What? he asked, waking from his daydreams.

—Yes, she said, you just didn't recognize me. It took you long enough, I have to say, Christopher.

He gave her a look.

—I'm not so sure I have yet.

—Silly boy! she said. Ember of the god, meet ember of the goddess. Only she didn't blow herself up. She has more interesting things to do. Though she sometimes needs her god to do them with. Is it not so, my lord?

He shrugged and smiled.

—Aargh! she growled gaily. When will you ever learn?

—Teach me, he said after a moment. Really. Honestly. Now. I want to learn.

—What?

—The lesson.

She looked at him hopelessly.

—If you don't know by now, who can teach you?

She turned sharply to him.

Her frown indeed looked just like that of the little girl in his daydream.

A cenotaph for his grave. Taps played on the horizon. An ashtray gripped firmly in her hand. The feeling of the blood moving in low thumps through his veins, as he had felt that time in hers. He could feel it now in his neck, when he placed his fingers there. Soft as a drum. Quiet as the grass, as a tree growing, as a hawk rising toward the height of the sky like a little black boat on an ocean. He marked the silence behind the owl's shriek, the wolf's howl, the cicada's shrilling in an August night, the chirping cricket, the sweetly cluttered singing of sparrows as the sun rose. A silence blind as the moon and deep as the sun. People couldn't stand it, it was quiet enough to make one go mad, so they made a racket to prove to themselves they were still alive.

—Am I wrong?

—You're always wrong. But it's too late to take back what you said. Even an erasure is a kind of dishonesty. A word once spoken. Is always spoken. The damage is done, the bone's broken. It's cruel and unjust, but there it is. The devil held his tongue in his hand. And yanked it hard.

—There's a lesson for you.

She looked away with growing contempt, though he was not sure for what or whom.

A chip of paint fell from the ceiling to the carpet. It was white and small, shaped roughly like the state of South Carolina, a triangle with one side curved like a hull. The ocean washed one border, the forest spread from the other, a mesh of roots and leaves, trunks and branches stretching across the land, the trees messaging each other, speaking, listening. The forest covering, protecting the ancient, nearly primeval soil. From what? you ask. From whom?

But the question gives itself away.

—From you and me, she said, in the tone she used to drive a point home: harsh, clipped, slightly baritone. Then she said, to no one in particular, as though she had just surprised the thought inside her: I don't want to be human anymore. People change their sexual identity with a few operations and six months of behavior therapy. They change their national identity by taking a test, reciting an oath, signing a document, they change their religion with a few mumbled words and a dunk in a baptismal font. DNA exchange is all the rage. So why must I consider myself "human"? Why is that so necessary? What is so wonderful about being human anyway? Not only are we making our planet uninhabitable, we are ugly, vulgar, selfish, ignorant, bullying, cruel, arrogant. Did any creature better deserve to be destroyed? Or abandoned? I hereby renounce my species, I hereby renounce my place in the human race,

I hereby become an animal of unknown species, part fish, part reptile, part insect, part bird, with the head of a cat, the body of a lizard, the tail of a wasp and the wings of a hummingbird. I will have the soul of a dog, loyal unto death and forever howling at the moon. I am even willing to give up my wonderful brain—it was the human gland for generating thought that got us into this mess. The human brain cannot save it, it will only make the horror it created worse with its self-immolating solutions. I renounce it all. I give it up. I will give up my humanity to save my shame if not my life. To be human is a disgrace.

He listened, only mildly shocked. After all, it was like hearing his own thoughts spoken back to him in a tense, quiet, feminine voice. Making the words seem all the more shocking. It had been coming for some time. Her vehemence was all the clearer in the quietness of her voice, her eyes' veiled shine, her hands that had not moved from her lap. As he watched her, she seemed to turn into the creature she had just described, and the room filled with the sound of her wings.

The dim cowering into dimness. You were leaving the human behind you. And with it both the angelic and the demonic. Even the divine, for who without us would have dreamed of God? Your sublimest creation, your dream of a supreme creator, all good, all powerful, all knowing. Your metaphysical guarantee. You would slip back into the feral out of the gaudy prisons of civilization, the compulsive disgust of modernity, the gradual suicide of the industrial and its idiot savant son, the technological, revolution, the perversions of capitalism, its obscenities, the legal mass murder of war, the hysteria of the internet, the slow brain death that is democratic culture—that long failed experiment called humanity. You would close this chapter with an ellipsis—who knows what would follow? You would move into the world's past.

He could feel the cortical functions burn out, one by one, like short circuits, drawing a curtain gradually over his brain. Memory would be the first to go, as in a kind of controlled dementia, the verbal functions, the ability to make connections, to plan, abstractions would vanish in a cloud of sensations, numbers volatilize like comets between the orbits of the planets, the final loss would be imagination, sad magic now without a purpose, it would disintegrate in the acid of perpetual sensation and the relentless procession of dreams, instinct would invade action like an army of moths, fur would cover his cheeks, feathers rustle his belly, a beak harden between his perfectly round eyes, his hands metamorphose into talons, his feet grow claws, and wings sprout from his back like a falcon's. Like Gabriel's or Lucifer's.

But he would be no Gabriel and no Lucifer, only animal again, innocent in his violence and hunger. Anything to escape being the monster clown, the giggling obscene predator called man.

—But what if we're missing something?

—We're human, how can we expect anything less? We're always missing something.

—Yes, but what if we are missing the point our humanity made possible?

He gave her an ironic look. For a change.

—Have you changed your mind?

—Listening to you (she said) has a perverse charm. But what stops me from quaffing off a beaker of DNA-decoder, mitochondria and ganglioside-decoupler, is the thought I won't only lose the existential hypocrisy that so much of being human consists of, this house of lies I carry inside my cranium, but I will also lose the only truth I know.

—And what is that?

—That despair is also a lie. Maybe the biggest lie of all. Which is why it was always considered the greatest sin.

—Give me another. Cocktails are back in fashion this season, the classics—the martini, Tom Collins, gin and tonic, Manhattan, the daiquiri, the high-ball, the Margarita, the black Russian, the b-and-b, the brandy Alexander—and newcomers, flash-in-the-pans, nine-day wonders, instantly forgettable instant classics: the roto-rooter, the shrink's bill (you drink one of these, you never see a shrink's invoice again), the stone of Aran, the Absolut quickie, the purple penis, and the Peruvian Pisco surprise.

The portly man sighed.

Drugs of choice of an older generation: barbiturates, Mary Jane, LSD, dexies, heroin, meth, orange wedge, hash, speed, Duco-Cement—and those of a later, nervier, crasser, stupider, more self-destructive, freer generation: ecstasy, serafin, Ritalin, steroids, HMG, opioids, etc., etc. Anything to make you numb for a few hours: just conscious enough to blow your mind to bits and leave you staring at them, spinning just past the ends of your fingertips, twinkling, like the stars in your pocket, the galaxies sticking to your feet like sand, the dust dancing an endless merengue in the summer twilight of your dilating eyes. Ecstasy! That's it! Keep pouring it, Maxman, let the suds pour across the bar, over the floor, rise to the ceiling, flood out to the street, muck up the traffic for miles, cause chaos across the city, douse fires and traffic lights, stuff malls and subway tunnels and high rises and overpasses with its pale, fragrant softness and finally roll in great white frothing billows like a thick foaming fog across the endless bar counter of the horizon. Pour it, man!

•   •   •

—Why can't you be kind? Even your enthusiasms are poisoned with sarcasm. Nothing must be praised without irony, loved without conditions, admired without reservation. There is no wrong you don't remember, vividly and in detail. Of the evil of humankind one can indeed say "it hath no bottom," to quote the rude mechanical.

You will be of that kind because that is all you can be. Slavery, war, slaughter, the wiping out of societies, of species, were considered, by the members of their societies, part of that thing before which everyone must bow: the demands of God, the orders of the king, the unavoidable thing called "reality." What wrongs are occurring now, of which you know nothing, because "we must do our duty, obey God, face reality"? God, history, evolution, the economy demand it: the elimination of the Indians, the slavery of the blacks, the extinction of a dozen species a day, the leveling of nature for a maximized return, the persecution of the Christians, the extermination of the Jews.

—You're becoming preachy again, says an unknown voice. Readers don't like that.

I know. Look up. What's that scent? Beyond the roses, the lilacs, the sweet bank of honeysuckle, what are those heaps in the field, burning? What is that strange fragrance? What are those distant yells, those cries, that sound of sobbing? The silence that followed was worse.

She followed his eyes for a moment where they stared in abstract sympathy out the window. She couldn't help suspecting his sudden flood of moral sensitivity; she always suspected hypocrisy or at least self-deception. Another passing lunacy. An attack of persecution complex. A spasm of ludic virtue, or a momentary lucid mania

And yet, she thought, God help us.

There was an edge of hysteria in her voice. She was stronger than she realized, but seemed to think her sensitivity meant she was weak. She was not, of course; she seemed to collapse easily, then rebounded with a speed, and a grace, that were sometimes astonishing. He, on the other hand, didn't seem half as sensitive as she, and it took a savage pummeling to make him collapse. But once down, he stayed down. Might stay down for years. And the consequences of his bitterness and hatred and lust for revenge could be very disturbing. She could recover (for example) from a broken heart, a romantic breakup, within weeks. And often did, as she had the habit of giving her heart freely, her kindness was so great (though heaven help you if you earned her hostility, which could happen as quickly, and for the most surprising reasons, as the winning of her affection). He, on the other hand, was as much a miser with his love as with his hatred: indifference was his usual gift to people, an indifference cloaked with impeccable manners, thanks to his upper-middle class breeding as a child. But if he fell in love, he loved to the point of despair. His heart did not break, it shattered. His few hatreds, curiously, never lasted long, or became diffused, as it were, politically: he felt a certain contempt for "humanity" but could never bring himself to dislike anyone into whose eyes he had ever gazed. The edges of his heart were soft with pity: everyone he met, even the wealthy, powerful, famous, seemed helplessly vulnerable behind a thin, transparent mask. They had no protection. They too were open to all the winds of peril and loss. The wind would take them whithersoever it listeth, as the phrase had it, despite their apparent strength, dreams of control, their fantasies of invulnerability.

Odd how things can strike you out of the blue. All you have to do is look up. And there you are, shaken and whirling in the wind.

A pool of darkness. To himself and his neighbors. A weeping willow above it, dragging its whip-like branches across the surface in the afternoon breeze. The little stone springhouse at the edge of the woods where they kept the cream sodas, the Oranginas, the cokes. The light gurgling of the spring over the rocks as it entered the pool. The olive green scum off toward the far side, where the tall reeds started in a dark green screen. The sound of a dragonfly darting past his ear, then the sight of it hovering over the pool, its whirring transparent wings, its delicately pulsing body as thin as a child's little finger; then it darts off.

The sense that a world of busyness is happening all around him, a hidden universe of intense, purposeful activity, from the grasses to the leaves, from the worms boring through the mud to the beetles and flies, to the lizards and snakes, to the squirrels, to the birds flashing in and out of the trees, to the little shifts of air, zephyrs, breezes, to the wind and the sky, to the clouds, the clouds, the clouds, those little worlds of chaos, to the sun, the unseen moon, the silent mob of stars behind the blank, opaque blue—in the apparent stillness, an endless busyness, motion endlessly rich, constant birth, constant renewal, an infinity of novel and strange and oddly beautiful forms, a panorama, a spectacle of beings he was, in effect, and maybe even in fact, blessed with witnessing and living among. A formation of fighters thunders across the sky.

One day an ant decides that all of creation has been made for it and it alone—from its creation myth in a clump of eggs in the corner of a damp tree stump, its growth, scrambling over its myriads of cousins, into maturity, its dramatic adventures scurrying over the forest floor, its toilsome existence dragging pieces of dead leaves and beetle husks into the darkness of its anthill, its heroic destiny as an ant-angel squeaking hosannas to an ant-god in a heaven full of fellow insects—and it toils at growing its anthill and ant society to ever greater heights and to ever greater glory, to prove its grand dreams were justified, that nothing is too good for it or for its fellow ants, and that the rest of nature exists to support it, and will be, if need be, sacrificed to its interests, its survival, pleasures, whims. That ant, in its little soul and clever brain, has even invented a weapon that, implausibly enough, could destroy not only its own anthill, and all other anthills in the world, in one fell swoop, but the entire forest, the surrounding countryside, the mountains, the sea— all of life on earth. Such a clever ant! Such a mighty ant! Such a naughty ant! And it might do so, one day, just to show that it can. It's just that smart, and on a bad day, just that mad.

—He said, I almost envy that ant.

She said nothing for a very long time.

Keenly. As he wheels back toward the beginning. Not that his story will be completed. Because no one's story is ever quite completed; after all, one's story doesn't end with one's life. The ripe, hard kernel of one's life, burned down to its essence, sends its roots into the future, just as he had been in large part knotted from a myriad of tendrils from the past—a myriad? millions, tens of millions, hundreds, thousands—beyond human counting, beyond the calculations of the quantum computers of the future—in a similar way, he sent a tendril out to combine again and fertilize the wet, dense earth of the future, "nature," that small part of it occupied by humanity, and "beyond," for lack of a better word. That was all the immortality you needed, whatever it was you thought you hoped for. His consciousness—a weak light in a universe of turbulence and dark matter, unidentifiable energies, undiscoverable dimensions, impenetrable universes—would at last go out (had that wet match ever been lit?). It had served its purpose: it had kept this over-intellectualizing primate alive for the time it needed to reach its conclusions, such as they were. The unconscious part of his being—far the larger, graver, more living, perhaps even more valuable part of him—it was called by some, still, "the soul"—would stretch into the bounty of existence, as eternal, as infinite, as eternity and infinity themselves might be—you can't know, though consciousness will never cease trying to know, in the very teeth of its endearing optimism.

In the end, your brain decided it was not knowledge it could depend on, but faith, not cunning but belief, not learning but dreaming, not certainty but doubt, the unexpected creator of hope. The illogic of the heart was the beginning of wisdom: the philosopher whose namesake you were had got it right. What they called "intelligence" was a magnificent servant but a brutal master: power drove it mad. He had learned to strengthen his mind as much as possible, though that had turned out to be little enough, in order to master it. A weak intelligence was precisely a masterful one, a tyrant and despot, the camp commandant of the soul. But the strongest intelligence recognized its limits; it bowed to the soul's sweetness, its oddities, its little, crazy smile, for it suspected that in the soul's quaint little madness was the deepest human truth—a truth you were always foolish to attempt to refute, because, no matter how often it was defeated and sent packing, it always returned, banners out, drums and fifes and trumpets sounding, like an antique army, against the high-tech military of the mind, the might of satellite, stealth bomber, nuclear weapon, special op, drone—and like the guerrillas of old, against the bloated, over-armed and arrogant, it always, though often only after a bloody and wasteful struggle, won. A single soul can overturn the world.

She still said nothing. You wondered if it was because she finally almost approved of what she was hearing.

—Crippled and lunatic and afraid of nothing. A man worthy of the name. That's what he was. They'll never find his like again. Though they will no doubt try. The fools!

The portly man smiled pensively into his almost empty mug.

—That doesn't sound too awful, do you think?
—Not on your life.
—Well, that's one way to put it. If we thought this was that, and that was enough, who in God's name would put up with it?

—I can't imagine. Or rather, I could, and that's what makes it so awful. Like the reactor melting down to the planet's core. Or the thousands of tons of water contaminated from cesium radiating the North Pacific. Or the spent rods, as they are carried down from the water towers, rattling and touching and exploding, raining, or rather snowing death, silent and invisible, without taste, without odor, across the islands of Japan, across the coast of southeast Asia, inland to China, north to Mongolia, to Russia, southward to Bangladesh, Pakistan, India, eastward to Afghanistan, Iran, Iraq, Syria, Turkey, Europe, the Atlantic, the Americas, a snow of invisible whiteness wrapping the world like a package for millennia.

He turned to her this time.

—The guy from the collection agency is on the line, and he's beginning to be abusive. I keep telling him they packed up out of here a long time ago, but he refuses to believe it. "They're got to be there," he said. "There's no other place they can go. They're hiding somewhere, that's all. Just keep looking. When you find them bring them to me. I can wait. I've got nowhere else to go. The bill just keeps growing—the miracle of compound interest! I've got all the time in the world." Then he hung up.

A stroke and shock and ache.

—The friend who, alone out of everyone in the world, understood you, laughed with you, forgave your foibles, your silences, your neglect, and smiled whenever he saw you—one day you turn to him, reach out to share a story, a joke, a little success or defeat, or just to catch up on news and gossip, and he's gone. You are surrounded by strangers, a vague wall of hostility, pity and scorn, the dead eyes of indifference, the mild disgust and giddy triumph the young feel for the old, and you realize that is how you once felt too, the only real wealth is time, and blessed and graced above all the middle-aged and old therewith, and how you knew it and strutted in your glory, your beauty, halo, pride. And the most glorious gifts of all that you had were your friends, who loved you, who you loved, without demands, at least in appearance, and that can be enough. How far away it is now, the irresponsible laughter of the young. You were not grateful enough. You thought they would always be there, ready to turn to you with a big laugh, a happy, welcoming smile, ready to share a laugh forever—after all, why not? Why not?

There is no answer to that question. It is not allowed. The roses die, despite your best efforts to water and weed, prune and protect them. Pets die despite your care, great trees die after genera-tions, civilizations die after centuries of grandeur and bloodbaths, species die after millions of years flourishing on the revolving earth, friends die a day after you had coffee with them and you parted with a laugh and a promise to call next week, after you have known them since childhood and assumed— assumed! you never gave it a thought—that they would last at least as long as you did, mortality acknowledged as an abstraction only, something that would happen "some day," but not tomorrow, not today. Today, with its annoyances and irritations, was secure, sacrosanct, safe. But then no longer: there comes, today, "some day" itself. It is like grabbing for something you always hold onto to keep your balance, and all your hand meets is empty air. And you almost fall. Or you do fall. And keep falling.

—Where are you now? Sasha asked him, as if he were deep in some hypnotic trance. I'm still here, she said. You don't have to be afraid.

—Yes, he said, I know. But for how long?

—How long will you be there? she asked, with an ironic smile. Where will I be if you go?

He laughed lightly.

—You've had your nice little bout of self-pity, it's time to dry yourself off and face the day. There's some heavy lifting to do. And just as there are more roses, pets, May flies, sequoias, species, civilizations to come, so there are more friends to make, even for old heads like you. To say nothing of current friends not to take for granted.

—It isn't all about me? He beamed, radiant. Damn all . . .

That had been a very happy day.

You couldn't escape. Like existentialists in love. Those mafia of philosophy. Who only kill their own. When they spent that summer in Sicily, Old Empedocles' island, when Syracuse was a goodly city and the great Pythogorean had walked the hills in his robes. And they were stumbling up the slope of Mt. Aetna, the volcano into whose mouth the old philosopher was reputed to have thrown himself at the end of his life, still smoking from a little recent, casual eruption, just to remind everyone it was still alive, when they came upon a peculiar piece of graffiti scrawled on a square, flat stone in ink or black paint or Magic Marker, the ambiguous phrase "KAOS i AMOR." As in old Empedocles' ancient doctrine of the origin and history of the cosmos, fluctuating forever between the poles of, on the one hand, love, wholeness, and order, all creation brought together in a tight embrace, and, on the other hand, chaos, strife, anger, all creation torn to pieces, before being pulled together once again by love, the process beginning all over again, without goal or aim, forever. It wasn't always unambiguously good to be pulled together by Love, because everything was then crushed together into a ball, a blob of pure entity, a kind of seamless, lifeless sphere, and it was Chaos, or Strife, that made possible having a universe filled with separate things: everything from galaxies to snapdragons, from space stations to iPads. Sasha and Pascal were only possible in a chaotic world, a world of strife and anger that was haunted by memories of the world of Love, and so they spent much of their time trying to rebuild that world in the midst of the chaos they knew, and which had made them possible. But once the world was ruled again by Love, everything would be squashed together again into a great ball, everything would be perfectly ordered once again, silent, still, perfectly comprehensible, but also, unfortunately, dead. And Love would be haunted by the memory of separation, of strife and chaos, of feeling, thought, sensation, life, all of which were only possible after the destruction of union, and the world would begin again to pull apart, out of the numbness of being into the suffering of becoming. And Chaos would break everything up again and create a charged, dynamic, exasperating, and incomprehensible universe.

And they read the graffiti and couldn't decide what language it was in, the peculiar use of "i," by itself and in lowercase, threw them off, so they played with various translations: "Chaos and Love," "I love Chaos," "I chaos Love," "Chaos I's Love," and whatever else came into their heads, for every possible and impossible, plausible and implausible meaning, and then they played with which one of the pair of them might be "Chaos" and which one "Love," and sometimes Pascal was Chaos and sometimes he was Love, and sometimes Sasha was Chaos and sometimes she was Love, and the cosmos spun out between them in its endless dance between the two poles, never settling at either one but always moving away from any settled state, in a perpetual state of chaos and love, strangely like human life itself, which can never stop at either love or strife, of the love that binds or the self that frees, but must forever destroy itself to go on. And then Sasha had a question: what was the relationship between Chaos and Love? Because (putting on her philosophical cap) that relationship defined Empedocles' cosmos more completely than either love or chaos did alone. Was it love, or was it strife? Or did it change as well; was it sometimes strife (when the cosmos was in the state of Love) and sometimes love (when the cosmos was in a state of Strife)? Or was it something else entirely? And so they played long into the summer evening in the hotel in the ancient town near the base of Mt. Aetna in Sicily as it erupted in a small way, rumbling under their feet just enough to remind them that the world under their feet was not perfectly secure. A plume of volcanic ash rose like a long gray feather above the kaldera at Aetna's top, and bent toward the east, scattering ashes into the Mediterranean.

—Chaos and Love, said Sasha. The philosopher and the whore.

—Which philosopher? asked Christopher.

—You can do better than that! Sasha crowed.

—Not Nietzsche.

—Ach nein, meine kleine Schmetterling! she riposted with a giddy, shocked look. Norman Vincent Peale!

—How could I forget. But who is the whore then?

—Mrs. Miller. Julie Christie would be so proud. She played her, you remember, opposite the young Robert Redford.

—Chaos himself.

—And they toss the world between them, forever and ever. Chaos, mon amour.

—Love, what a gas!

Between the bordello and the snake-oil wagon, the ad man and the parvenu, the social network and the stunt man, the chief evangelist and the black site, the special ops and the fraudulent mortgages, Caedmon and Machiavelli, the Venerable Bede and Gilles de Rais, Gilead and Hermann Kahn, the big heat and the big short, the destitute past and the catastrophic future.

—Between thee and me.

A step a step. Then another. And another. Wherever we are going. Not knowing where. Not knowing when or how or why. Just going. Like a character, if it can be called that, in one of the Irishman's stories, if they can be called that. A

Russian, an astronomer, a philosopher and a whore enter a bar. The Russian orders a vodka and bemoans the meaninglessness of existence. The astronomer orders a cosmo and says, with a shrug, "Who needs the meaning of existence when you've got an entire universe, with its billions of stars, to explore with your telescope?" The philosopher orders two shots and a beer and says, "You're both pathetic. Vodka's the meaning of life for you, Ivan. You're only happy when you're moping. And you scientists are all alike: you think the world, truth, reality, actually exist. What you call the 'universe' is nothing but a projection inside your own head. And that telescope of yours? It's just a neurotic substitute for your little Johnson." The whore asks for a ginger ale and says nothing. After a moment, the Russian, the astronomer and the philosopher turn to her. "Well? What do you have to say for yourself?" She looks at them and then takes another sip of her ginger ale. "I really like ginger ale," she says. The philosopher nods sagely. The astronomer smiles: the bubbles in the ginger ale remind him of the stars. The Russian softly moans to himself. The whore shrugs and takes another sip.

The winter covered an unknown world with an impure but haunting whiteness. If he could only discover what it was. A step a step. And end the insanity of reason. That you cannot escape. A modicum of sanity was all you needed. A stroke and shock and ache. Such comfort even in the cold. That doesn't sound too awful, do you think? Though I would seriously consider rephrasing that line. Crippled and lunatic and afraid of nothing. A falcon hovered above the tower. Keenly. But he was not desperate enough. A pool of darkness to himself and his neighbor. Make them stand on their own feet. You don't believe me. But love had nothing to do with it, as the song put it. Why can't you be kind? That's exactly what I mean. So give me another. That abrasion of the mind. The dim cowering into dimness. Sound typical? She turned sharply to him. It was really wonderful to see. A pale tide. Though that might be too much to ask for. Though he may have been wrong, of course. But they were. If only you could be good. Don't fool yourself, he said. Yes, let them levitate at will. My home is elsewhere. Be careless and free. It was a delicious sensation. Dewpoint. It could be a lifetime. All because of the photographs. A little bit of phenomenon. From the old country. Unquiet grave. And what about you? The prevailing winds. A short spell of heaven. Ocean. The gods make us suffer so we'll make better music. The tang. But it didn't anymore. Pity was a rich source of contentment for him. Because hope was its own reward. The smell of the future was in the air. So they tell me. Life being a joy at first before it was a pain. She felt so much better afterward. But that meant nothing. Wake up, wake up, no, no, go back to sleep. It was without, let's say, a certain heroism. He lacked the courage and character for that. Called adulthood, if you remember correctly, that curious fraud. Free at last. Like existentialists in love. And other spectres.

—Marry me, he says.

Her eyes open wide.

—No! Chris . . .

She bends down, folding her arms in her lap, burying her head in her arms. She is wearing the soft burgundy robe he gave her for Christmas. He quietly strokes her auburn hair and repeats, Marry me . . . And again: Marry me.

—No . . . She shakes her head over and over in her arms.

At last she raises her face to meet his own, and he looks at the little nose that had always so moved him, it is so like a child's, and the raven brows, and the wild lips, and the austere cheeks that, when he first met her, had thoroughly intimidated him. They are slick with tears.

She's laughing.

—Well, he says, suppressing the quiver in his voice. As I said: I am in love with you. He casually picks up the coffee pot. But I don't love you.

And throws

No.

... She is smiling.

He throws his arms wildly around Sasha's shoulders, vulnerable as a pair of shorn wings, and crushes her lips against

No.

She is crying.

—Damn you Chris damn you damn you damn you if only you

No.

—I told you. I love you. But I will never

No.

—I despise you, you fatuous narcissistic God how

No.

—I don't know what to

No.

He says nothing for a minute, nodding as though agreeing, or merely signaling he has heard. Then stands up as though finished with breakfast. Takes hold of the coffee pot, as if to pour himself another cup of coffee.

Instead, he raises the glass pot and brings it down with a savage motion against the back of . . .

The sound of the wind shaking the windows fills the room.

Shortly afterward, he leaves for The Liars' Cafe. The brightness of the snow is almost blinding.

Or this:

Leave it as it is. Without resolution. The two of them paralyzed at the breakfast table, frozen as in a photograph. Neither of them knowing the answer to the questions each has made of the other and of themselves. Waiting for answers that might never come. Answers without which they cannot live. Or even die, for that matter. And yet answers they will never be allowed to have. Like life itself, sometimes. Or often. Or always.

Perhaps the answers are lurking somewhere in the story told so far. If so, they seem to have missed them. And now they will think them through obsessively until, like tire marks in mud driven over and over again in an attempt to pick up another track, they have become completely effaced.

The last thing you hear is the wind shaking the windows.

And they disappear into the darkness of this imagining.

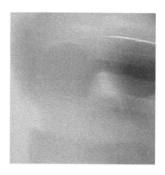

Christopher Bernard's previous books include the novels *A Spy in the Ruins* and *Voyage to a Phantom City* as well as collections of short fiction and poetry. He contributes regularly to *Synchronized Chaos* and is co-editor of the webzine *Caveat Lector*. In 2019, he was awarded the Albert Nelson Marquis Lifetime Achievement Award.

CPSIA information can be obtained
at www.ICGtesting.com
Printed in the USA
FSHW020929060719
59699FS